Also by Andersen Prunty

Bury the Children in the Yard: Horror Stories

Pray You Die Alone: Horror Stories

The Driver's Guide to Hitting Pedestrians

Sunruined: Horror Stories

Hi I'm a Social Disease: Horror Stories

Fuckness

The Sorrow King

Slag Attack

My Fake War

Morning is Dead

The Beard

Zerostrata

Jack and Mr. Grin

The Overwhelming Urge

FILL THE GRAND CANYON AND LIVE FOREVER

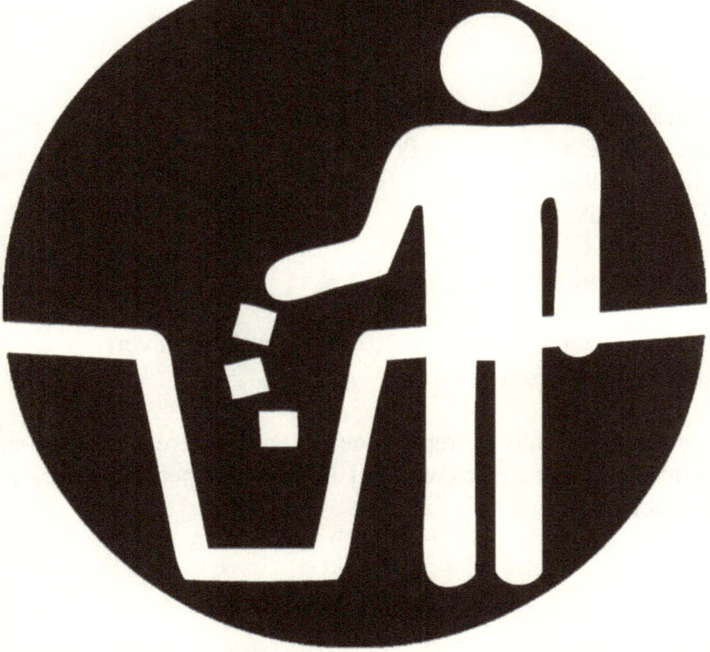

ANDERSEN PRUNTY

ATLATL

www.atlatlpress.com

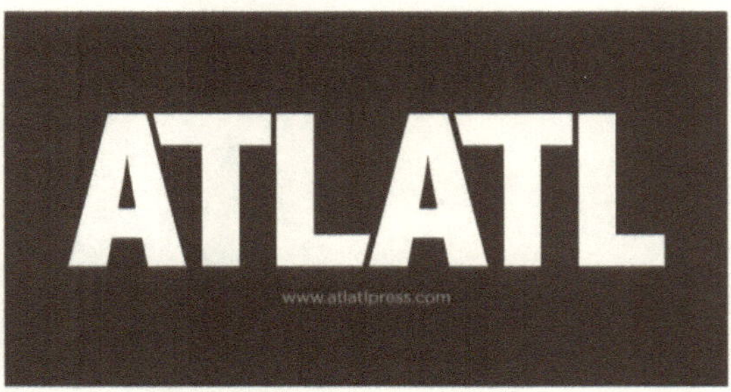

Scary Places Are Best Left Outside

I'm in a scary place. I have been for nearly a year. It feels like my head is filled with fog. I sit on the couch and watch TV. A thin old man is talking about the Grand Canyon. It sounds like he hates it. He's calling for people to fill it ... I think. Nothing is really that clear to me right now but it sounds like a great idea.

Sometimes the house is filled with people. Most of them I don't know or, if I did know them at one time, I've since forgotten them. Maybe they're not even real. Much of the time, like now, the house is empty. It's either empty or the people are hiding in the shadows and holding their breath.

The TV flickers. The man continues to talk about the Grand Canyon while the fog continues to eat my brain. Agatha sleeps upstairs. Maybe she's doing something else.

I grab my laptop and go to MyFace. I have ten friends. I know three of them. MyFace has this great feature that allows you to start a real or imaginary group. I check to see if there's a group of people who want to fill the Grand Canyon. There isn't. I start one. It's great. It takes about three minutes. I have a glowing sensation inside my head and for just a second I think of the sun burning away the fog. I wonder if I should have made it an event instead of a group. But all events have an end. I wanted this to be something that could last forever.

I Stayed Behind

The week after high school graduation my friends decided to take a trip to the Grand Canyon. I was going to go with them. The night before we were to leave I had a terrible nightmare. I stood on a promontory overlooking the Canyon. My friends were there, Greg Handel and Brandon Henson. They made me feel like my last name should have started with an "H". They were really happy, jumping up and down. I was nervous. A fall would be catastrophic, but I could feel the Canyon sucking at me like a vortex. Greg said, "Watch this. I'm having a great time," and jumped over the edge. He wore a t-shirt that said: BAD DIALOGUE. I wanted to watch him fall through all that red brown space but didn't want to get any closer to the edge. Then Brandon said, "I really like to jump," and leapt off, leaving me alone on the promontory with that sucking feeling. I wanted to jump but I was too afraid. I turned to move away from the edge, to more solid ground. Felt left out of something.

Snakes, a lot of them, were blocking my way. I think they were coral snakes. The poisonous ones. There's a rhyme to help remember which the poisonous kind are but I couldn't remember the rhyme. Behind the snakes, a bear, ferocious and snarling. I had two choices – bear and snake combo or the sucking void of the Canyon.

I woke up with a deep sense of loss and called my friends. Told them I couldn't go.

I stayed behind.

It's been over a decade and I haven't seen or heard from either one of them.

I stayed behind.

I'm still here.

With Agatha. With a series of cracks and holes filling my brain.

Agatha is either my wife or my roommate. I vaguely recall getting married a year or more ago at a bar in Las Vegas. That may not be accurate. Regardless, we sleep in the same bed and sometimes I think we have sex but she could be lying to me. That is, the vagina might not be real. It might not be her. It's usually dark.

She has another sleeping partner who she calls Buddy but I think he's more than that. I think she's having an affair. He's been in bed with us the past two nights. I'm not sure if he's had sex with Agatha or not.

I try bringing this up to her even though I'm not sure I care. We're in the bedroom. Buddy is sprawled out on the bed on the other side of her, naked and snoring, one hand cupping his genitals. I put this question to her casually as I check the MyFace page for Fill the Grand Canyon. I still only have ten friends but this page has a thousand fans. Who knew?

"Not here," she says. "Let's go downstairs."

I grab her wrist, suddenly aroused. I want to drag her back to the bed, push her face into the pillow, pull her sleeping shorts and underwear down just past her ass, and hate fuck her while Buddy continues to sleep. Or wakes up. What would he do? Maybe that's why I want to do this. To see what he would do. I know what I would do. Nothing. It's what I've done so far.

She yanks her arm away and gives me a look. Points a finger down.

We go downstairs. She points to the closet and says, "There's the closet. Why don't we go try on coats and talk about this later."

I follow her to the closet. She pulls out all the coats and piles them on the floor. She's wearing a green t-shirt with yellow block lettering that says: TITS across her chest. We try them on. I take off each coat before putting on the next. She just layers them. Most of the coats are too tight for me but she's able to get most of them on at the same time, as though her torso is contracting with each coat.

"You've gained weight," she says. "You look like a gorilla."

"You're really wearing a lot of coats."

"Because I can. You could only wear like one coat. Barely. Fatso."

"That hurts."

"I can't be with anyone this sensitive. I think I need to go."

"What do you want from me? I think something is eating my brain." I imagine a canyon forming in my brain. What's that thing that separates the lobes? That's some kind of canyon, isn't it? I used to imagine my brain as a smooth white globe with things rolling around inside perfectly, sometimes hitting and bouncing off each other but they never escaped and nothing ever got in. Then there were the cracks and holes. Now I imagine them combining to form this massive canyon.

"I need to go." She repeats this while I'm not even looking at her but staring somewhere just over her shoulder and thinking about my brain.

She leaves the house. I watch her disappear into the night. I shut the door and go upstairs next to Buddy and fall asleep.

The phone rings. Buddy stops snoring and barks out like he's in pain, like something terrible is happening to him in his sleep. I answer the phone.

"Hello."

"This is Estelle."

"Hi Estelle." I don't know anyone named Estelle.

"I feel wild."

"You sound really old."

"I'm like sixty-five or eighty."

"Jesus."

"Yeah." She sounds orgasmic.

"Can I help you?"

"I wanna get sick and nasty."

"That's pretty gross."

"That's *just* what I want."

"Okay."

"Want me to come over?"

"I'll meet you."

"On the corner?"

"Sure. On the corner. Do you know where it is?"

"Oh yeah."

"Hot."

"You bet."

Fill the Grand Canyon and Live Forever

I hang up the phone and wonder if I should tell Buddy I'm leaving. I guess it doesn't really matter. I don't even know why I'm leaving. The phone call seemed strange. I probably should have told her she had the wrong number after she gave me her name. She didn't seem very concerned though. So why should I be concerned? Will she be expecting someone else? I head out to the corner. It's chilly outside and most of the houses are abandoned. There are many dogs barking. Barking and barking and barking and it's late at night but the birds haven't started chirping yet. A car roars down the street and screeches to a halt at the corner. It's something gigantic and dark colored. Maybe a Cadillac or a Buick. Decades old. The door swings open, scraping the sidewalk. Estelle hops out. She's dressed inappropriately. Slinky lingerie and fishnets it looks like she bought at the stripper store. Her white hair is curled tight.

"Hey," I say.

She stumbles around on her high heels, drunk, and shouts, "Get in the car, Porky!"

I do what she says. The door's really heavy. The door itself is bigger than a lot of cars. The interior is covered in wood. Ashtrays are everywhere, most of them overflowing. My life feels meaningless. I've been given nearly three decades to make my own choices and this is what it comes down to – following orders from a drunk old lady because whatever she has planned is better than what I had planned, which is nothing, which is lying in bed next to the man who was probably fucking Agatha and wondering how many people would like my MyFace page.

"You know," I say. "I'm not really that fat. I'm only about twenty pounds overweight."

"I don't care." She seems really angry.

"It's just ... you called me Porky. My wife left me because I was too fat, among other things. I have really low self-esteem. No real sense of purpose. Maybe a brain tumor or something. What you said did nothing to help any of those things."

"I was talkin about that fat cock. I call all my boys Porky."

"Oh ... okay. Hey, is that a wig?"

"This?" She points at her head.

"Yeah."

"It sure ain't my real hair."

"Well, I mean, is it like a wig or did you scalp somebody?"

She peels out from the curb. "Wig." Her wrinkly mouth draws tight.

"Can I try it on? I really like wigs."

She grabs it off her head and throws it into my lap. I put it on and bend the mammoth rearview mirror to look at it. I look ridiculous. I like it. She drives over a possum the size of a child and laughs. I laugh too. Estelle's fun.

She lights up a really long cigarette and passes the pack over to me. It has a smiling horse on it with the word "Magic" written across the horse's stomach. I light one up and crack the window.

"So what're we doing?" I ask Estelle.

"I told you I feel wild."

"I know but I don't know what that entails. When I feel wild I get scared and think the best thing I should do is take some deep breaths or maybe a nap or something."

She makes something that might be a smirk but with all the wrinkles in her face I can't really tell. She doesn't say anything. I try to turn the radio on and she smacks my hand away and tells me if I try to do it again, she'll burn my face. Without her wig she looks ghoulish and creepy. Eventually we're in an even worse section of town. She pulls the car into the parking lot of an all night grocery store and kills the headlights. The grocery store is lighted in a way that makes it look terrifying. I don't want to go in. It has one large window in the front but it's too dirty to see through.

An old man walks out of the store. He's wearing a black t-shirt that says: RABBIT HOLE in white block letters. He isn't carrying any bags or anything and I think this seems strange. Estelle guns the car, blasting the headlights. The man's eyes widen and his legs bend as he begins his attempt to dive away but the car hits him, throwing him up onto the hood and over the roof and we're out of the parking lot and speeding along an alley behind the grocery store and there are trashcans full of fire and hollow-eyed men leaned up against garages and the moon shines overhead and we're both laughing and laughing and laughing and then Estelle digs a claw-like hand into my thigh and says, "Give me back my fucking wig."

Morning in a Strange Land

The blue dawn slants through the window and the sound of birds is everywhere. I'm lying on the floor. My skin feels crusted over and I'm very cold. I struggle to stand up. Old people are lying passed out all around me. The stench of something like burning carpet stings my nostrils. I have to get out. My chest feels tight. I feel like I've done something horrible. I look for Estelle. She's in the corner, slumped against the wall, her shoes off and her lingerie twisted around her. Her false teeth are jutting from her mouth, a string of drool connecting them to her wrinkled chest. I nudge her with my foot. She snaps awake.

"I need to go," I say.

"You can take my car. Keys are in the purse." She waves her hand toward a gigantic orange purse.

"Thanks."

I rifle through the purse until I come up with the keys. This smell is really bad. It makes me think there might be a fire somewhere in the house or apartment or wherever. I cross what I think is the living room but end up in another room almost exactly like it except there aren't so many people on the floor. There is only a man in a wheelchair laughing and pointing at a small television. The only thing on the screen of the television is something in block letters that says:

PLOT IS A CON

I open the door to this room and it leads to the outside and a wooden landing that begins a steep and rickety set of stairs. It's even colder outside and I wish I had a jacket. I forget exactly what Estelle's car looks like and all the cars parked on the curb are huge. Most of them are unlocked. Some of them are filled with horrible things and stains and smells that come from some kind of insane underworld.

I finally find Estelle's car and fire the engine. There is a blood stain on the windshield and I remember the man we hit in the parking lot last night. I wonder who he was. Before pulling away, I get out of the car and remove the license plates with a survival knife I find in the glove compartment. There's hair or fur or something in the teeth of the saw on the opposite side of the blade.

I head for what I hope is home. Last night is hazy. I'm not exactly sure where I am. I'm not at all sure of what happened last night. We went back to Estelle's place and she reached into her gigantic purse and pulled out a bunch of pills and said, "Here take these," and I did and then I kind of blacked out. I think I remember chanting at one point in the evening. There may or may not have been a man there wearing horns. It might have actually been the Devil. I don't believe in the Devil. But there was chanting and an orange strobe light and there might have been a sacrifice.

I'm shivering in the car. I turn on the heater. I turn on the windshield washers to try and get some of the blood off. I can never remember a time when cars were this large. Maybe when I was a very small boy. But that might have only been because I was so small and everything seemed larger.

Some memory suddenly washes over me and I remember being in high school, sitting in the passenger seat of Brandon's car and two amazingly beautiful and absolutely ripe girls sat in the back seat and we were all smoking cigarettes laced with marijuana and laughing and the world seemed vibrant and alive and open and stretched out before us. And I wonder what happened to that feeling. I wonder what happened to my best friend. I'm on the verge of crying so I turn on the radio. It's an episode of *Fresh Air* and Terry Gross is interviewing cancer and I think that doesn't really help very much.

Maybe I should go home and get my car before going to work. Maybe I should ditch this car.

A block away from my house I pull Estelle's car into an abandoned house's driveway, cautiously look around to make sure no one is watching me, and get out, leaving the keys in the ignition. I walk home with my hands in my pockets and wonder how many fans the Fill the Grand Canyon page has.

I get close to the house and see Buddy standing in the front yard in his underwear, his breath pluming out from his mouth. A girl dressed in a black and white cheerleader's outfit stands in front of him. There is a skull and crossbones emblem on the outfit's top. She is crying and he is stroking her cheek with the back of his hand. She's holding one black pompom down by her knees. He kisses her on the forehead and she walks away, stopping to shove the pompom into the sewer before catching a bus that stops at the corner. Buddy waves as she gets on. He looks hollowed out and sad.

He's wearing a blue t-shirt that says: NOT FROM AROUND HERE in wild tropical colored letters. He looks at me and says, "It is cold."

I don't know that I've ever heard him speak before. He sounds robotic.

"Agatha took all the coats," I say. "Who was that?"

"Girl."

"What's her name? She's quite attractive in a slutty jailbait kind of way."

Buddy stares at me and doesn't answer. Maybe he's not a robot. Maybe he's from a foreign country and just doesn't speak English very well. He turns and goes into the house. I follow him. I need to grab my keys. I go upstairs, thinking maybe I'll take a shower to try and get this crust off me. Buddy is already in bed. There's a trail of blood leading into the bathroom. I weigh myself, sigh, and hop in the shower. When I get out there is no towel. I let the steam out of the bathroom and walk through the freezing upstairs. I can't find a towel anywhere. I briefly imagine Agatha even larger, even puffier, wearing all the coats and stuffing them with towels. I use a dirty t-shirt to dry off and then get dressed. I glance over at Buddy and notice he is using all of the towels to cover himself. I wonder how I can get Buddy out of the house.

I go downstairs, open my laptop, and check the Fill the Grand Canyon page.

100, 000 fans.

Amazing.

I have nine friends.

Agatha has unfriended me.

I shake my fist and growl. Imagine her wearing all those coats and nothing from the waist down. Imagine my fist in her vagina up to the wrist. Imagine cracks, holes, and canyons and remind myself I have to go to work so I can make money to feed myself and things.

Raccoon

Someone has broken all of the windows in my car. The stereo has already been stolen so they took the passenger seat and replaced it with a mutilated raccoon, probably roadkill but, given recent events, possibly a sacrifice. I open the passenger side door, grab one of the many fast food bags on the floor, and remove the raccoon. I think about shoving it down into the sewer but decide not to. This way the raccoon's family can find it and give it a proper burial or perhaps a cremation.

The drive to the elevator factory where I work is freezing. I stop at McDonald's on the way because I'm really hungry but also kind of sick and think McDonald's will either fill me up or make me vomit. I once ate McDonald's every day for a month trying to win their Monopoly sweepstakes. I really need a million dollars. I need to stop working at the elevator factory. I need to start playing the lottery. A few years ago I self-published a book called *Dick Swap* about two guys who ritualistically trade penises but, when one of the penises goes missing, an absurd bromance of epic proportions ensues. So far it's only sold twelve copies and I haven't written anything else. It's *not* making me a millionaire. I haven't even recovered the amount it cost to publish it in the first place.

I order the number two and eat it on the way to the elevator factory. I take a deep breath and go inside. I'm only an hour late today. I feel good about things.

Working in the Elevator Factory

The elevator factory towers fifty stories into the air. There is only one floor at ground level. The height is just an elevator shaft. There's a warehouse part where blue collar men assemble the elevators. The rest of my coworkers are just people of various weights who take the elevator to the top and then ride it back down. Everyone wears a nametag with his or her name and weight. We have to weigh ourselves weekly in front of the HR person, Linda 158. The women seem more upset about this than the men. There is a group of men who've turned their girth into a competition. They can barely move. Their goal is to be the only one the elevator can support. I'm Andy 189. I used to be Andy 165 but this job, along with lack of and subpar sex, has made me fat.

Occasionally there are fatalities. My job is mostly to answer the phones and also clean the restrooms, which I don't like to do and haven't done for a very long time. When I go inside, the office manager is waiting for me. Her name is Candy 256. She looks like a man in drag. She tells me the boss would like to see me. I go back to his office and he opens the door and he's not wearing any pants and his office smells like shit and I see actual piles of shit on his floor and I know it isn't going to be good.

Mr. Elevator

But it is good. In fact, it's great.

"Andy, dude, come in and have a seat." Mr. Elevator says things like dude to make himself sound younger. He also does things like flash me the hang loose sign when we pass each other. No one does that anymore. It's either refreshing or terrifying, like he's out of his head or out of touch or just really happy.

I inspect the expensive leather chair for human waste before sitting down and crossing my legs. I try not to stare at the piles of shit on the floor or the half-empty bottle of scotch resting on the corner of his desk which explains both the looseness of his stool and the especially cloying vapors filling the office. He sits on his desk in front of me. He has a lot of pubic hair shaved in an interesting fashion. He stares at me with his mouth open.

"What's up?" I ask.

"In the world of elevators, everything is up ... And then down."

"Of course."

He takes a slug from his bottle of scotch, misses the desk on the return, and it shatters on the floor. He waves a dismissive hand.

"You ever heard of Dubai?" he says.

"Yes." I think I have.

"Well we've got really good news." He's practically shouting. "They're building a hotel that goes up into space and they want us to provide the elevator. They're paying us in gold. That means a raise for everybody!"

I smile and say, "That's great news, sir."

"As you can see I've been shitting in my office." He motions to the nearest pile of shit. "And ... I think that has something to do with you but ... why are you here?"

"Candy said you wanted to see me."

"To tell you about the raise, my man!"

"I'm very appreciative. My wife left me. I might have a brain tumor. The writing career is not going well. Someone is stealing the seats out of my car. This will help with the mortgage or rent or, well, I haven't got that figured out yet. She handled everything—"

He's just staring at me and nodding and I decide to quit talking. I stand up and leave thinking eventually he'll remember why he called me in there and that it probably has something to do with the piles of shit and I don't really feel like dealing with it.

Back in the office I take a phone call because I see Candy staring at me from her desk and know she's probably going to want me to do something horrible and answering the phone, even though it means talking to someone who probably has a really stupid problem, seems like the lesser of two evils. It's a person calling from somewhere overseas. I can't really understand them. I get the gist of it. Someone is stuck in one of their elevators. One of *our* elevators. And apparently has been for a couple of days. I tell him we just build and install them and ask if they've notified any sort of emergency services. He tells me that it's our name on the elevator and therefore we must deal with it. I tell him we will and hang up. I'm not going to do anything. I breathe deeply, trying to center myself, and stand up to go outside and take a break. Candy is standing right behind me. She's stealthy even though she looks like someone who should squeak when she walks.

"What'd Mr. El want?"

"Oh, you know, he just wanted to chat."

"You're full of shit."

"Bowels." I don't know what else to say.

"Speaking of shit ... Have you visited the restrooms lately?"

"Of course. I clean them like every day."

"The ladies' restroom is *awash* in menstrual blood. I don't even want to know what the guys' restroom looks like."

"Spotless." This is probably a lie. Thirty guys use the same restroom. It has one toilet, one urinal, and one sink. I stopped going in there roughly a week after I stopped cleaning it. That was about three weeks ago. I imagine what it must look like. Pubic hair and man splatter everywhere.

"I can smell it all the way out here."

"That's something else."

"It's your job. It's like the only thing you do."

"I was getting ready to go on break. I'll take care of it when I come back."

She trundles back to her desk. I go outside. One of the guys from the back is squatting down in the grassy area behind the parking lot. He's holding a newspaper and there's a roll of toilet paper to his right. I get in my car and drive home. I'll tell them I got sick if they ask. Eventually someone else will clean the restroom. On the way home I notice a billboard usually carrying an advertisement for *The Super Slutty Teen Show* now bears only one word:
COMPLICIT

I Have Always Wanted a Best Friend in the World

The rest of the drive home, I wonder what I'm going to do about Buddy. I decide I'm going to act like we're best friends. I'm going to tell him I'm dying. Maybe I'll tell him about the Grand Canyon thing, even though it's only a MyFace page. That should strengthen the bond.

True Bros Brush Their Fucking Teeth Together

I'm so excited by this revelation I don't even bother shutting the front door. Buddy isn't downstairs so I rush up to the bedroom. He's still in bed. The towels are all thrown off him and he's wearing only his white briefs. I don't want to make him feel weird so I strip down to my boxer briefs and jump beside him on the bed, playfully prodding him.

"Hey, bro, wake up!" I say.

He rolls over. He's really groggy. I notice he has a mustache for the first time. I grab a pillow and hit him with it, not too hard.

"What ..."

"Yeah, bro, it's time to get up. Wanna go downstairs and watch *Man vs. Food?*" I hit him with the pillow again.

"Brush teeth."

"Yeah, man, we'll brush our fucking teeth together."

I rush off to the bathroom, grab all the toothbrushes and toothpaste and a glass of water, and for the next few minutes we are putting toothpaste on toothbrushes and some of it is spilling on the bed and we're both smiling and brushing the holy fuck out of our teeth and there's water everywhere and I feel like we've established some kind of bond that will make our coexistence something peaceful and long lasting.

Even though the house is freezing, neither one of us bothers putting on any clothes. Buddy takes a bunch of pills that are in the nightstand and I go around the house opening all the blinds, letting the sunlight in. It's early afternoon and school must be letting out because there are yellow school buses everywhere and dog faced children running down the sidewalks, laughing and tackling each other, throwing cell phones like footballs, texting wildly, clothes either so tight they might as well not be wearing any or so large they're flapping in the breeze and encumbering movement. And they're all saying "fuck" and "shit" and "pussy" as loudly as they possibly can. I think to myself that civilization has ten years, tops. But I still feel good. I got a raise. I have a new best friend. The sun is out. The kids are partying.

I turn on the TV and the closing frame of what I'm pretty sure is a snuff film flickers across it before the word DANGER appears in red block letters on a yellow background. I click the TV off. I'm covered in goose bumps and remember that I forgot to close the door. I notice a folded piece of paper lying on the floor just in front of the frame. I unfold it. It says, in palsied handwriting: "I had a really great time last night." And it's signed "Estelle" with a phone number under it and at the bottom is either a lipstick kiss or a dirty anus mark.

I'm not sure I want to pursue this thing with Estelle. She seems aggressive. I wish Buddy would come downstairs so we could eat bagels, drink beer, and give each other fist bumps.

I go to the bottom of the stairs and shout "Buddy!" repeatedly. Then I feel stupid. He probably thinks I'm retarded. Then I remember something Agatha said about retarded people only being here for people to laugh at. She was very cruel. I wonder where she is now with all those coats. Probably Alaska. I wish I lived inside of a bear.

Buddy comes downstairs. He's wearing his underwear and a t-shirt that says: PROGRESSIVELY DUMBER.

"Hey, cool shirt. Is that a band or something?"

He stares at me. Buddy really rocks the mustache and wears it with no irony whatsoever. I'm not even sure he knows what irony is. I think about growing one but I think my mouth is too small. My father always had a mustache. I never saw him without one. It made me distrust him. He eventually drowned himself in protest of children.

"What took you so long? I'm afraid *Man vs. Food* isn't on anymore. I would have DVRed it but I couldn't find the remote control. I can't even remember if I *have* a remote control."

"Blood mouth."

"Aw, man, did we brush our teeth too hard?"

He points into his mouth. I get up close and look in, stick the tip of my index finger against his mustache. He has a giant sore on his tongue. It's bloody.

"That looks bad," I say. "It almost looks like cancer. Do you want to go to the doctor?"

"I will just sit down." He moves over to the couch and sits down. I fight the urge to sit on his lap.

"Yeah, just sit down there on that comfortable old couch."

I move to sit down next to him but he quickly sprawls out, taking up the whole couch. He stares at the ceiling. It occurs to me that, even though I've been acting out of character for me, my brain tumor might be imaginary. Buddy seems way sicker than I do. I don't have any open sores anywhere. Thinking he's dying makes me want to befriend him even more.

"I know it's rough as fuck being terminally ill and shit. I'll go to the store and get some beer. I'll buy a six pack and make them put each can in a paper bag. That way we'll have six paper bags. And then I'll come back and we'll drink the fuck out of that beer. But first I need to put on some clothes because it's cold outside and I'm only wearing my underwear." I'm talking really loudly now. Holding my hands away from my hips, palms out. Possibly just talking to hear myself talk but it feels like my ears are clogged up and there is a ringing somewhere deep inside my head and I imagine my brain lined with the same kind of sores as the one on Buddy's tongue and I think it's possible we're both dying but I feel really energized and I just want to go outside and run around the block in my underwear until I can't run anymore. I put on my clothes and try to fist bump Buddy on my way out but he's already asleep so I just bump my other fist and then do that thing where you open up your hand and waggle your fingers to simulate an explosion. That's what Buddy and I will do. We'll rampage and explode through the world like only two terminally ill guys can.

Drinking with Buddy

I can't buy beer from the first place I go into because there are like fifty people inside and I get really scared because they all have camouflage faces and are wearing t-shirts with dead deer on them and brandishing Bibles and talking about why no one should buy anything from terrorists and that Mexicans are taking all of our jobs and everything they say seems really nasty and self-interested and the Indian clerk looks more afraid than I am and it all just seems too heavy.

The next place I go to is better. The woman cashier gives me bags for all the cans without asking why and when I ask if I can have bags for my hands, she gives me those too and even calls me "Hon."

I rush home to Buddy, surprised to find him awake. He's watching a documentary about the Grand Canyon and looks terrified. I find myself briefly mesmerized. It's like the Grand Canyon is following me around. I feel like getting drunk and calling someone, asking to hear all of their theories about the Grand Canyon. I tell Buddy maybe we should change the channel. He changes it to static, which is something I haven't seen in a while.

"I got some brewskies!" I shout because the static is up very loud. I take all the beers out of the bags and throw the bags around the room. I crack open a can and hand it to Buddy. "Let's pound the shit out of these!"

He's trying to choke down the first one but it's probably really hurting that sore in his mouth. I'm on my third one before he's even half-finished with his. He says, "Agatha," and looks sad and I realize I don't know how to respond to that. After all, she's my wife. Maybe. Then he says, "Bed," and I tell him it's not even dark out but he's going up the stairs and I pound two more beers and think about finishing his but I imagine that it's full of gross tongue sore germs and I just leave it because I don't want to catch his cancer but now the static on the TV is even louder and I feel like doing something, I feel like exploding, so I pick up the phone and call Estelle and just as I'm saying, "I really want to see you," the static on the TV fades and is replaced by a commercial for guilt.

Estelle tells me we'll burn down the world and I wonder if that's what I want. I check the page for Fill the Grand Canyon. 500,000 followers. My confidence soars but it feels kind of hollow, like it could plummet any minute. But I don't feel like this very much so I embrace it, try not to think about what might come later, and ten minutes later Estelle rips through the front yard in a Jeep with vanity plates that say "2DEEP."

Estelle blares the horn and I start climbing into the Jeep when she tells me I have to sit in the back because Clarence is in the passenger seat. I don't see anyone but I do what she says. She seems really on edge. I sit in the back and wonder why the top has been removed from the Jeep and really wish for the millionth time that I had a coat. She rips through the side yard and bounces into the alley. We drive through a series of alleys. I never realized Dayton had so many alleys but it seems like a half an hour before we're on any type of main road. And then it's only to bound up onto 35. My arms are wrapped around myself and my teeth are chattering and the speed of the highway isn't helping at all. By the time we reach 75 South my blood is finally pumping and I'm starting to feel less like a corpse.

"Where are we going?" I ask, knowing I should just enjoy the ride but, given my past experiences with Estelle, I know wherever we're going could lead to savagery and horror. I think I'm okay with this.

"Clarence has a cane!" she yells. Spit mists out of her mouth and spritzes my face. It smells like Listerine and death.

"What!"

"Clarence! Has! A! Cane!"

"Great!"

"And it has a skull on it!"

"Clarence sounds like a badass!"

"What!"

I repeat myself but it doesn't elicit any response. The rearview mirror frames Estelle's wild eyes. We're in the fast lane and doing well over a hundred. There are very few other cars on the highway. She stops and tells me I have to drive.

"I don't want to drive."

"The arthritis in my knees is really fucking with me. Get behind that fucking wheel or I'll cut your face."

She slides over into the passenger seat.

"What about Clarence?"

"Clarence got out a half hour ago. He's a limp dicked motherfucker. By that I mean he's my son and I have had sex with him."

"Therefore you know all about his erectile dysfunction and his penchant for relations with mothers."

"The next time I hear fancy talk like that I'm biting your ear off. Get this bitch moving. It's stolen."

I slam on the gas. Eventually we pass a stadium-sized church fronted by the skeleton of what used to be a giant Jesus until it got struck by lightning. I think, Jesus was a cyborg. Estelle stands up and unbuttons her top. She's not wearing a bra, her nipples extend to her waist, and she bounces around. "Look at these, Jesus!" she shouts. It's just like Mardi Gras.

"Drive faster!" she says. She's still standing up, her breasts and loose skin flapping in the wind. I try to turn on the heat and she karate chops my hand away.

We pull off an exit somewhere in Cincinnati. She spits directions at me and I robotically maneuver the Jeep until we're in front of a dilapidated Victorian house. It's the only house with any lights on.

Great! Maybe she's taking me along to another one of her parties. I really wish Buddy were here. Estelle hops out of the Jeep and winces. She buttons up her floral-patterned polyester church dress and I realize how conservatively she's dressed. She goes around to the back of the Jeep and grabs a couple five-gallon cans of gasoline.

"Grab those." She points at a couple of road side flares.

"What are we doing?"

"We're having fun. We're making the night glow. We're aging and regressing." Then she growls at me and lashes out at my cheek with a claw. It hurts. I think it's bleeding but I'm holding these flares and too preoccupied to check. We walk up onto the porch. She sets down the gas cans and tries the door. It's locked. She tells me to kick it in. Says it'll be a blast, a really big time, a fiesta, arena rock.

I kick the door several times. I can't kick it open. I'm chubby and weak and not a master of kicking open doors. The door opens anyway and an old man stands on the other side.

"Why the banging?" he says.

Before he can say anything else, Estelle throws herself on him like a wild cat, gouging his eyes, kneeing him in the groin.

"Grab the gas! Splash it around!" she says.

And the next few seconds are filled with people screaming and running from the house and I'm splashing the gas all around the perimeter of the room I'm standing in, the fumes enveloping me, and I'm having a really good time and immediately want to move to another house and do it again. I look back at Estelle and she's continuing to rip at the poor old guy's face and when he seems immobilized she grabs one of the flares and sparks it up and tosses it into the room. I run through the open door and head for the Jeep. Estelle's limping along behind me, silhouetted in the hell orange glow of the house. I sit in the passenger seat. My hands are shaking. My nerves are shot. I can't possibly drive. And I begin to wonder if what I just had, what I just experienced was, in fact, fun. Or was it just something I felt and I'm confusing that for fun? Or did I just do whatever Estelle wanted me to do?

Estelle gets behind the wheel and we swing through another series of alleys and then we're at a parking garage and we're driving to the top of it and then we're out of the Jeep and standing against the concrete barrier and Estelle is pointing at the burning house and mouthing the word, "Beautiful."

I think of the mutilated man inside, rolling around on the floor and screaming.

Estelle moves a hand with knuckles the size of walnuts over my cock. It's unresponsive. She reaches into her giant purse and pulls out some pills and tells me to take them so she doesn't have to rip out my tongue and I do it.

In a few minutes I'm rock hard.

She crawls up onto the hood of the Jeep, hikes up her skirt, and slides down a huge pair of underwear.

She says, "I'll let you wear my wig."

She says, "You'll have to get the lube out of my purse. You'll need a lot."

She says, "Yeah, that's it."

She says, "Yeah, just like it's 1939. I'm the magic paper bag."

She says, "Fill me while the world burns."

She says, "Faster. Harder. You need to lose some weight or you're going to break my hips."

She says, "Come on my tits. Spray em with that shit."

And I'm doing everything she says and I'm looking at a lighted sign beyond the Jeep that says ROOF and has an arrow pointing up and the light is blinking and then it's going dark and we're lying in a puddle of grease covered with a crocheted blanket that smells like mothballs and gasoline and I ask, "Who was that man?"

Cosmic Dust Needs Vacuuming

I'm still wearing the wig but my shirt is off and my pants are down around my ankles. She lights one of those long cigarettes and hands it to me before lighting another one for herself.

"Don't ask me questions like that."

"And the guy from last night—"

She presses her cigarette into my thigh and I bark out in pain. She exhales a languorous blue plume.

"Besides," she says, "you only want to know about them to make yourself feel better. You think if I had a good reason to do what I did then you could feel like they deserved it and then you would feel less guilty. Let me tell you some things. I'm a product of the Depression. Everyone my age is a product of the Depression. We grew up with nothing but when we became adults we had the opportunity to give our children almost everything they wanted and we did that. Mostly material things because those were exactly what we didn't have. And then they grew up with everything and wanted more and more and gave their children—people like you—everything. But you wanted more. You wanted to feel important and special so they had to give something else to their kids. Attention. But a parent's attention is never enough so they had to make you feel like everyone else paid attention to you too. Like anyone cared. No one cares. They've never cared. We are all just a speck of cosmic dust."

Preachy, I think. And then say, "But why kill other people? If we're all just specks of dust, why not just leave people alone?"

"Because some dust needs vacuumed up."

"You're so nihilistic."

"I am nothing. Yours is the generation that wants to be labeled. But you're all just consumers, really."

26

I take a drag from the cigarette. "I'm just fat and sad and ... cold."

She stands up. "You're bumming me out. You can get your own ride home."

She snaps up the afghan and before I can even stand and pull up my pants, she's in the Jeep and speeding away and I wonder if I'll ever see her again.

She forgot to take the wig so I leave it on for warmth. I can't find my shirt anywhere. I wish I had a cell phone. Agatha has a cell phone. I need a pay phone. I wonder if pay phones even exist anymore. I wonder what I said that set Estelle off. She seemed bitter. She's probably the angriest, most bitter person I've ever met.

I begin walking down the ramp of the parking garage. I'm really far up. I find a staircase and take it, thinking an attendant who sees me on the ramp might have some questions or something. I don't think it's a crime to wander through a parking garage. I'm pretty sure it's a crime to light houses and people on fire. I'm also pretty sure I still smell like gas.

The stairwell is brightly lighted but it has a really odd smell to it. A few stories down I come across a man bundled into a sleeping bag. I stand over him for a second. There is an atrocious smell wafting up from him. I wish it was Buddy. Maybe this homeless person could be my friend. Maybe he's not really homeless at all. Maybe he just likes sleeping in parking garages. I just had sex with a really old person in a parking garage. People do stranger things. I prefer to think that's what this guy's doing. It's just an experiment. He has a warm home and a loving family to go back to and he doesn't have any mental problems or addictions or anything. This is how he has fun.

I nudge him with my foot.

He pulls down the sleeping bag and tells me he thinks he's going blind. Then he becomes defensive and asks me what the fuck I want.

"Do you have a phone?"

"Yeah, I gotta phone," he says. "Do you need to call the President?"

"No, I don't think so. I need to call someone to give me a ride back to Dayton." Then I think maybe this isn't really true. I don't really know many people and those I do know don't drive.

"You wanna take a ride in my sleeping bag?"

"Are you inviting me to have sex with you because, if you are, I have to decline. I just had sex up there and then she left me. That's why I need a ride."

"Damn bitch."

"That's a misogynistic statement and a really derogatory term."

He mocks me like a child would and pulls out his phone. I'm glad "phone" wasn't code for something else like drugs or his shoe or his dick.

He says, "Let me update my MyFace page first." He stands up and wraps a smelly arm around my shoulders and we both smile into the phone and he takes a picture but it doesn't flash because it's already so bright in the stairwell. Then he types in something and hands me the phone.

"What'd you type?" I ask.

"New friends. LOL."

"Super."

"Who you callin?"

"Well, first I'm going to try my wife or my ex-wife or my former roommate and then I'm going to call my BFF Buddy. He's a standup guy but he has a chemical dependency problem and he might even be dying of cancer so I'm not sure he'll be up for the drive. He sleeps a lot."

"I'm gonna take a piss."

"All right."

The guy pulls down his filthy pants and begins urinating onto his sleeping bag.

I call home. It rings and rings. Maybe Buddy is still sleeping. Maybe Buddy is having sex with that sad cheerleader I saw him with this morning. Maybe Buddy is dissolving a person in acid in the bath tub. Jesus. Buddy wouldn't do a thing like that. That sounds like something Estelle would do. The voice mail prompt comes on and I say, "Hey Buddy, this is Andy. I'm in the Nati and need a ride back to Dayton. If you can help me out in a couple seconds give me a call at this number. Otherwise maybe just, I don't know, drive down I-75 or something. Man, fuck it. I don't want to be a pain in the ass. Just forget about it." I press END and call Agatha. It rings and rings. I imagine her phone in the bottommost layer of coats and give her a while to get it. It doesn't go to voice mail or anything. Just rings and rings. I hand the phone back to the possibly homeless guy and say,

"Thanks." I search in my pockets until I find a dollar and hand that to him too.

"Thanks, man. God bless you."

"Yeah, right."

I wander around town until I come to a bar called Aluminum Can Drinks. There is a cab in front of it. Why didn't I think of calling a cab? I walk to the cab and hop in the back.

"I need a ride to Dayton."

"That's far away."

"I know."

"I can do it."

"Thanks."

He pulls away from the curb. The ride is completely uneventful. The cab is warm. I sleep all the way home. When I get home it's just before dawn and I go upstairs and get in bed next to Buddy.

A Head Full of Many Negative Thoughts/Dan Banal Opens a Box

I awake mid-morning to the sound of a chainsaw. Buddy is on the far side of the bed. The sad cheerleader lies in between us, staring at the ceiling. Her thick eyeliner has run down over her cheeks like she's been crying or sweating. My head is full of many negative thoughts. Last night did not go well at all. I think I hate Estelle. Or maybe I'm just afraid of her. There's probably a big difference. I get out of bed. I'm still wearing the wig, although it's slightly askew, and I apparently never managed to find a shirt. I don't know why the cab stopped at all. Maybe it was stopped for somebody else. I look down at the sad cheerleader but she doesn't make eye contact, just blinks slowly, her arms crossed over the skull on the front of her top. I walk over to the window to see what all the racket outside is. Not surprisingly it's a man with a chainsaw. He's dressed like a lumberjack and sawing at one of the remaining trees on the street. It creaks and then crashes into a neighboring house. The lumberjack looks at it and nods. I expect somebody to come out. Admittedly, there's a part of me that wants to watch the impending conflict but none of that happens. The lumberjack wanders down to the end of the street and disappears around the house on the corner.

I look at the sad cheerleader and say, "I'm going to go down and make some coffee. It will be black and strong and you're welcome to have some. I'll probably also eat a bagel and check my MyFace page."

Still staring at the ceiling, she says, "No one talks like that."

I want to respond but I can't think of anything. I want the sad cheerleader's vagina in my mouth. Something still feels screwed up in my head. I imagine even more cracks and holes. Maybe a black hole or something that leads to another dimension. I notice Buddy is lying in a pool of blood and the sight is horrifying. What if something really bad is happening to him? But ... maybe that's the sad cheerleader's problem.

"First I'm going to find a shirt."

I walk to the closet and grab the first t-shirt I can find. Every t-shirt I own is black. This one is too tight but I'm too lazy to take it off and find one that fits. I think my gut is sticking out the bottom of it. Probably repulsive. I go downstairs to do what I told the sad cheerleader I was going to do.

I'm not sure if I have to go to work today or not. I pick up the telephone but it doesn't make any kind of sound. It's possible it's been disconnected. Agatha always paid the bills. She had it fixed so we never got anything in the mail. She did it all over the Internet but I never bothered with it so I figured I would just stay in the house while everything slowly shut down around me and then I would probably have to move. Or find somebody else who knew how to do things. Estelle seems like somebody who knows how to do things but she's also really old and maybe not my type.

I go into the kitchen and put some coffee on. It smells really good. While it brews, I fetch my laptop. Maybe Agatha has sent me an email detailing the bill situation. I imagine her sitting in a library somewhere, bulky and confined beneath all the coats, trying to maneuver her arms over a computer keyboard. Impossible. She doesn't care that much.

I open my laptop. No legitimate emails. Spam for dick enlargement, pills, and things bordering on child pornography. I decide to check my Amazon ranking for *Dick Swap*. It's ranked really low. That's really bad. Then I check my MyFace page and notice I have a friend request from Chuck Barrymore. I recognize his profile picture. It's the homeless guy from last night. He's used the picture he took for his profile. I feel briefly flattered and think "Fuck yes" before accepting the request. I check the Fill the Grand Canyon page. It has 750,000 friends. Someone has a left a comment that says, "Juts trew my washing masheen in!" This makes me feel even better about things. I think, Making friends and filling up the cracks and holes. I close up the laptop, pull my many copies of *Dick Swap* off the bookcase and lie on them until the coffee maker beeps. *Dick Swap* is currently the only book in the house because I had to sell all of my other books to finance the publication and purchase of so many copies. I thought at least people at work would buy them before realizing I was too embarrassed to try and sell them something called *Dick Swap*.

I pour a cup of coffee, grab a bagel from the bag, and take them into the living room. Sitting down makes my stomach bulge against the shirt, makes it feel even tighter. I turn on the TV. There's a sweeping panoramic view of the Grand Canyon and my stomach lurches, my head swoons, and I almost black out. Overlaid on the sweeping vista is the word FREEDOM. Bullshit. I change the channel as fast as possible, scrolling through until I land on *Dan Banal. Dan Banal* is a sitcom about a man named Dan Banal. The show is just starting. There's nothing exciting about this show at all, except lots of people watch it. I don't watch a lot of TV but, admittedly, I enjoy *Dan Banal.* The opening credits are not set to any music. They're just words over a slowly panning shot of Dan Banal that starts at his brown tasseled loafers, taking in his baggy pleated khaki pants, brown leather braided belt, blue button-down shirt, completely plain face, and modestly styled hair. He wears the exact same thing in most of the shows unless it is set on the weekend. Then everything is the same except his hair is slightly messier and he wears an untucked red and black flannel shirt.

The show opens with Dan bringing in a cardboard box from the front porch. He places it on the table where his wife, Lori, sits reading a newspaper.

"We got a package," Dan says.

"I wonder if that's the printer," Lori says.

"Let's see."

Dan goes into the kitchen and opens a drawer, pulling out a box cutter. He opens the package at the seams, walks back into the kitchen, puts the box cutter away, and comes back to the package. He opens the box.

"It's the printer," he says.

"Oh good," Lori says.

He lifts the printer out of the box and sets it on the table. Then he goes back into the kitchen to get the box cutter again, opens the bottom of the box, and puts the box cutter away. He flattens the box and walks it out to the recycling bin. He comes back to the table and stares at the printer. He grimaces.

"Where do you think we should put it?"

"Probably near the computer. It's a printer."

"This is a wireless printer. We could put this printer anywhere. Anywhere there's room."

"Wireless?"

"A wireless printer."

"Does it have batteries?"

"Doesn't need them. You plug it into the wall. This printer runs off electricity."

"That's hardly wireless."

"What it means is it doesn't need to be attached to the computer."

"But it has to be plugged into the wall ... with a wire."

"That still allows us a lot more freedom."

Dan reaches out and runs a finger along the surface of the printer.

The sad cheerleader comes downstairs and says, "Jesus, I hate this fucking show."

"No. It's pretty good. It's just like real life. Real life on TV is great." I take the first bite of the stale bagel but now that the sad cheerleader is in the room, I feel fat and self-conscious. I put the bagel between the couch cushions.

She stands there for a minute staring at the TV before crossing the room and turning it off. Looking at the sad cheerleader, I realize she's actually a lot more fun to look at than the TV. So I stare at her. She doesn't look necessarily clean but she is young and attractive. I find almost anyone under a certain age and weight attractive. Black hair cut in an experimental fashion. The cheerleading outfit is something I'm not really into but it's black and white and has a skull on it, so it's okay. And the skirt reveals a lot of thin leg and kneecaps. She's not wearing any shoes and her feet are not hideous.

"Like what you see?" she asks, maybe sarcastically, before adding, "Jesus."

"You turned the TV off."

"I told you I hate that show."

"There are probably other things on."

"I hate TV."

"Okay. There's coffee in the kitchen. I don't think there are any more clean cups. You'll have to drink it out of the pot."

"I hate coffee."

"Okay."

Awkward silence. She looks so sad. Almost ready to cry.

"I'm worried about Buddy."

"Me too."

"The only reason I come over here is so he can fuck me."

I sip my coffee. She's really open. I don't say anything.

"He wasn't even able to do that this morning."

"I'm ... sorry?"

"You should be. Would you mind fucking me?"

I don't really have to think about this. "Now?"

"Yeah, I'm going to have to catch the bus soon."

"Okay." I put my cup of coffee down on the floor.

She gets down on her knees and bends over the couch. I undo my pants. I haven't even washed since having sex with Estelle. It doesn't look like the sad cheerleader's offering oral sex so I guess it doesn't really matter anyway. I get down on my knees behind her and slide her black underwear down to her knees. She's already wet and my penis isn't very large so I slide right in and quickly build to a good rhythm. It doesn't take long before I'm tired but I can feel myself building to a climax and the sad cheerleader seems to be moderately enjoying herself so I keep going.

There's a noise upstairs. It sounds like Buddy has rolled out of bed and is now dragging himself across the floor. This kills the orgasm I was building to but I'm still slightly hard so I keep going. I can hear him thumping down the steps now.

The sad cheerleader says, "Faster. Faster. Jesus, I hope Buddy doesn't have cancer."

I go faster and the orgasm is back. It sounds like Buddy has become lodged halfway down the stairs. He's moaning. I pull out and pump my cock with my hand, unleashing a small amount of come onto the sad cheerleader's ass. She pulls up her underwear and sits on the couch. She's crying.

"That was really nice," she says.

"Thanks. I thought so too."

"I guess I should check on Buddy."

"Maybe. I should probably ..." But I don't really know what I should probably do. Maybe go for a walk. I think about asking the sad cheerleader if I should put glue into my head through one of ears to help seal the cracks and holes but instead say, "So what school do you cheer for?"

"I don't cheer for a school. I'm an independent cheerleader."

"What does that mean exactly?"

"It means I'm not confined. It means I'm free."

"Free to ..."

"Cheer wherever the fuck I want. Malls. Jails. Restaurants. Funerals."

"You cheer at funerals?"

"Most of them need a good cheerleader."

"All right. Hey, do you want a copy of *Dick Swap*?"

"What's that?"

"It's a book. I wrote it."

"Sure. Whatever. You can give me one but I probably won't read it."

"That's okay. Nobody else has."

I stand up and walk into the other room. The books are still on the floor. I pick one up and toss it to her. She's not looking at me so it just hits her in the chest. She cries harder. I think about her breasts, which I didn't get to see. I can hear Buddy moving again. I feel really guilty. I think the sad cheerleader is his girlfriend or something. So I think of years later when I'm telling this story to another set of friends and I have to tell them about having sex with my best friend's girlfriend while he was dying of cancer. I grab my cup of coffee and walk outside.

You Are a Comatose Lion

Estelle's standing at the end of my walk with a crowbar. I panic and throw my mug of coffee at her. It misses and smashes on the ground.

"Come here, you little shit," she says. She looks bad. Like she's been up all night and even older than usual. I remember I'm still wearing her wig. I throw that at her too. It doesn't even make it there. She comes toward me and bends down to pick up the wig. "Come on. I got something I need you to do for me."

"You were very mean to me last night. I had to take a cab back."

"You deserved it. You know you did. You don't have the magic feet. You are a comatose lion."

"I really thought we were developing something."

She's too close for me to stop her now and she moves around behind me and presses the crowbar against my throat. "Are you going to help me or not?"

"I'll help you. What are we doing? I don't know if I feel like killing anyone right now."

"You haven't killed anyone. We were just correcting the balance of things. Vacuuming up the dust, remember? Just a little housecleaning."

"I don't feel like cleaning right now."

"This is something different."

I follow Estelle. I think she's walking to her car or another stolen car but she just keeps walking. Over two blocks and up to a house and I have exhilarating flashbacks from last night but she just opens the door and walks in and this house looks and smells just like an old person's house. Not anything like that apartment she took me to on the first night. The one with the burning carpet smells and the passed out old people everywhere. There's part of me that wishes this is

Estelle's actual house.

Once inside she flops down in an armchair that looks at least sixty years old.

"Kyra will be here any minute."

"What do you want me to do?"

"I'd like you to go into the kitchen and talk to Don. Don's my husband. He's a maker of stars. He has strong hands."

The doorbell rings. "But first you can get that, you little fucker."

I open the door. A pretty young blond girl stands on the porch. She is holding a book. It isn't *Dick Swap*.

"Is Estelle here?" she asks.

"Yes." I turn to look behind me to make sure Estelle is still here. She makes a threatening gesture with her finger across her throat.

"I'm here to read to her." The girl holds up a trashy paperback. It's the really sleazy kind where the author has a completely fake name with an "X" in it. It's called *Passionate Frenzy*. The girl notices the way I'm looking at the book and says, "It's what she likes."

I retreat into the kitchen. Don is in there. Maybe.

I hear the girl say, "Who was that?"

"That's my grandson."

"Why doesn't he read to you?"

"He's retarded, honey."

I suppose this could offend me but I'm distracted by possibly Don and trying to fight the urge to either scream or vomit or both. I could stand there and open my mouth to scream and the vomit could fly out. I wonder if it would be possible to do it at the same time. But then that would probably make some noise that Estelle would take the wrong way and hurt, possibly even kill, me for. I don't even know if this *is* Don. I've never met Don. It could probably be anyone. There are a lot of bones clogging the kitchen sink and strips of skin hanging from the ceiling. Blood drips slowly from the skin and this makes me feel a little better. If it were partially rotting, I don't think I could help but puke. Then I would have *had* to try screaming while puking. I look for an exit but the one door in the kitchen and all the windows have been boarded up. So I stand there horrified and unable to do anything. I can hear the girl reading from the book. The book is really really filthy. Exactly the kind of thing I can imagine Estelle liking except I wonder why she isn't reading herself. I've seen her drive so I know she's not blind. Maybe she's just really farsighted or has some cataracts or something. Maybe she's just letting this girl read to her as some type of community service. But that doesn't really seem like Estelle at all. She's probably getting off on it.

After about a half an hour, the girl stops reading and says, "Well, that's the end of the chapter. Might as well stop there. Do men really like to put their ... things there?"

"All the time, honey. All the time. But it's good for a girl too. You won't get pregnant for one thing and if you still believe in saving yourself for marriage you can consider yourself saved cause they're really just talking about the pussy."

"Oh. So ... you said you'd bake some more of those brownies for me if I came back."

"Was that all I said?"

"No. I've got it right here."

I go to the door to see if I can tell what the girl is talking about. I'm hoping Estelle isn't trading sexual favors for reading. But the girl is giving her money.

"Boy!" Estelle shouts. "Bring that plate of brownies in here."

I was so distracted by Don I didn't even notice the brownies. They're sitting on the table. I bring the brownies out. The girl grabs one and devours it. Then she grabs another one. Her pupils grow very large and she slumps back onto the couch. She stares ahead of her with her mouth partially open.

"Now Kyra. Do you think your friends would like some of these treats?"

"Oh yeah." Her speech is slurred.

I start to say something and Estelle makes that threatening gesture at me again.

"I'll give you these treats and you can give them to your friends. How does that sound?"

"Sounds wild. I bet it'll cost a lot."

"I'll let you take this plate of treats for *free*. But the next time you want some treats, you'll have to pay me a little something for them. How does that sound?"

"I'll pay whatever."

"Well, you won't have to pay quite as much as you've been paying but if any of your friends want any, you should charge them what I've been charging you. That's called making a profit. How does that sound?"

"That sounds beautiful."

"My grandson loves my treats, don't you?"

I don't really feel like being drugged but before I can say no, she's threatening me again and saying: "He likes to sit right on my lap and let me feed them to him." She pats her lap and I'm sitting in it, careful to avoid sitting on her breasts, and she's raising a brownie in one gnarled hand that still smells like gasoline and blood and shoving it into my mouth and then another one and then another one and then I know it's going to be another insane night and I'll be lucky to remember any of it.

One of Those Creeps

I'm in a ditch by the side of a suburban street, on my stomach and vomiting into a puddle of puke that was already there. I try to scream but it sounds like gurgling. I note the perfect combination of screaming and puking as an impossibility. I'm only wearing underwear that it smells like I've soiled and I'm shivering in the morning cold and covered in dew. An attractive, clean-looking woman is holding a boy's hand as they walk on the sidewalk at the top of the ditch, probably on their way to school.

The little boy points at me and says, "Look Mom, it's one of those creeps."

She says, "Don't look at him. Just keep walking."

I want to stand up and say, "I'm not a creep!" but realize I'm staring at the woman's ass as she walks down the sidewalk—can't seem to focus on anything else—and know she's right. Maybe it's a residual from last night's drugs but I think about following the woman to her sterile home and peeling down her leggings and licking her asshole while masturbating. I wonder how long it's been since she's had her asshole licked. Maybe never. It probably tastes like soap. Especially this early in the morning.

I drag myself out of the ditch and try to orient myself. I'm only a couple of blocks from home. That's good. Maybe I can get home and take a shower before I have to go to work. Check the Fill the Grand Canyon page. I don't even know what day it is. I figure it's a week day or why else would that sweet ass woman be walking her jerky kid to school but I don't know that's where they're going. They could be going anywhere but, nevertheless, I feel a certainty they are going to school. Pre-school or kindergarten. Something easy and not even a whole day. Then I think that kid's a real loser. There's no reason for a kid not to be in school at least 8 to 10 hours a day. My father thought children should fuel the work force. Coming home from his factory job, he worked on a book called *Work and Learn* that proposed just such an idea. He never found a publisher. Possibly because, other than fathering one miserable child, he had absolutely no credentials save his burning hatred for children and childhood in general.

I'm still just standing there. I have to force myself to move. My whole body hurts. My stomach heaves again before I finally move on.

Old Friends Who Look Like Owen Wilson with Orange Hair

I'm walking up my porch steps and I see Brandon Henson standing with his back to the door staring out into space. At first I don't realize it's him because his hair is shoulder-length and orange and he kind of looks like Owen Wilson. I can't remember if he looked like Owen Wilson in high school or not. But I didn't know who Owen Wilson was in high school so that comparison would have been extremely prescient, if not impossible. I approach him for a hearty greeting and he backs away as much as he can until he realizes it's me, or at least that who I am is mostly unclothed and totally unthreatening.

"Brandon Henson! Man, it's been forever! Dude, you look just like Owen Wilson except your hair is longer and it's orange! Where the hell ya been! You look so fucking European! Mainly because of the way you're standing ... and the cut of your jeans and the way they're embroidered on the back pockets and have snaps on them! Hardly any dudes wear jeans like that here!"

He places a hand on my shoulder and says, "Calm down, man. How's it going?"

"Great! Awesome! Totally battle axe!" But inside ... I don't know. Things feel ripped up, torn apart, maybe burning. I wonder if I have an STD. Like maybe it entered my brain through one of the cracks and holes. Maybe I'm just stressed. With the dayjob, and the Fill the Grand Canyon page, Buddy's illness, his crazy needy girlfriend, Estelle, *Dick Swap*, it all feels like too much.

"Nice pentagram."

I don't know what he's talking about but he's pointing at my chest and at first I fight the urge to look down because I think maybe he's just playing that trick where you get somebody to look at something you've spilled on your chest and then they ... what is it they do? Hook your chin or something? But I'm not wearing a shirt and my chest really really hurts so I look down and see the bloody pentagram carved into the skin. Not knowing what else to say, I mutter, "Oh, thanks."

"Where are your clothes, man? It's kind of chilly. Not even summer yet."

I have horrendous flashbacks from the night before and don't have any way of putting these things I saw and took part in into words. I break down in great heaving sobs. Brandon pats me on the back and says, "It's okay, man. Let's go inside. Let's get you into the shower or something. Smells like maybe you've shit yourself. Do you care if I smoke some hash?"

I shake my head and we go into the house. The door isn't locked and a pungent stink wafts out. But now that Brandon has pointed out my stink I can't think of anything except showering. I go upstairs, Brandon right behind me. I notice Buddy is back in bed, wearing only a t-shirt that says: BILDRUNGSROMAN in gothic letters. Brandon follows me into the shower and I take off my underwear and he strips down and then says maybe he would rather take a bath so we run the water and smoke some hash while the tub fills.

How the Grand Canyon Ruined My Marriage

Brandon's cock is way bigger than mine and I'm really jealous. Smoke and steam swirl around the bathroom. The door is closed to keep it all in and make it a little warmer. The heat has probably been turned off too. Or just never turned up. I don't know where the thermostat is. Brandon gets in first with his back to the wall. That means I have to get in with my back to the faucet. Mildly irritating. The bathtub is really dirty. The walls around it are really dirty, too, stained black and brown.

"This is nice." Brandon closes his eyes and leans his head back against the wall.

"I haven't bathed in I don't know how long."

"I bathe pretty regularly."

"I usually don't take baths. I prefer showers."

"I *always* take baths."

"I've never taken a bath with a guy before. Feels weird."

"Feels great. Baths should be a communal experience."

"It made me uncomfortable to see your penis."

"I like sizing up the competition. Yours is pretty small."

I ask Brandon what he's been up to and at first he says he doesn't really know and then he says he moved to Europe after their Grand Canyon excursion. Not any place specifically in Europe. Just Europe. Like it's a city or something. Although he does mention the Eiffel Tower so maybe he's talking about Paris. Then he says he can't really tell me any more and asks what I've been up to. I tell him but I'm not really sure myself. I tell him about Dad drowning himself and how I thought it was really funny. I didn't even go to the funeral. I tell him about Mom in the asylum and how I never go visit her. And then I met Agatha and ... I don't know. There was Agatha and then there were the coats and Buddy. It seems like a lot more than that should have happened. But there are a lot of gaps. A lot of monstrous black spaces like the cracks and holes are devouring my memories. Thoughts continually drift to the Grand Canyon. Something happened there. I think maybe Agatha and I *did* get married in Vegas. Then took a trip to the Grand Canyon. Agatha liked it. She was like a thrill seeker, walking out on the ledges of the various rims. She said she wanted to build a house right there. She wanted to look out the bedroom window and stare straight down into the bowels of the earth. I couldn't go near it. She accused me of ruining the honeymoon. That was my first display of profound weakness. Over the next few months there were many more. But that was the beginning. I laughed and said someone needs to fill it in and that struck me as vaguely familiar, as a not completely original thought. I remember my fan page and, even further back, the old angry man on the TV. I probably need to get in contact with him. Maybe he's discovered the fan page already. Maybe he has a MyFace page. That makes contact so much easier.

Brandon's asleep and I think about drowning him. Drowning him and getting the hell out of the house to look for Agatha, to go the Grand Canyon, to do anything. I imagine leading a caravan of trash filled vehicles to dump in that pit of despair. I think about putting a call to action on the fan page. A manifesto even.

The bathroom door opens and the sad cheerleader enters.

"Cool! You guys are taking a bath. I hardly ever bathe and I'm really dirty. I think I can smell my crotch."

She looks even filthier than she did yesterday. Like she's been cheering in a dust storm or on the side of the highway or something. She's already stripping down. She gets in the bathtub between me and Brandon. Brandon is awake now. His erection has broken the surface of the water. The sad cheerleader's back is to me.

"I'm glad you guys were here. I thought I was going to have to jill off. Hi. I'm Persephone Pointless. My friends call me Phone like the thing you talk into."

"I always called you the sad cheerleader." But it's like I'm talking to no one, just staring at the knobs of her spine and finding them arousing. I think about wrapping my arms around her and cupping her small breasts. Maybe after she's clean I'll see if she's interested in putting her vagina in my mouth.

"I'm Brandon Henson."

"One of Andy's friends?"

He shrugs and looks guilty. "Something like that." He reaches his hands out and takes her small breasts in them. She moves back a little so her ass is pressing against my cock. She's kissing Brandon. Her head moves down and she takes him into her mouth. She's moved up onto her knees so I get on my knees and work myself into her. I can hear her gagging on Brandon but the motion causes her to tighten around my cock so I kind of like it. Water sloshes everywhere.

She pulls herself off Brandon's cock and says over her shoulder, "Put it in my ass so I can actually feel it." If I wasn't so high this would probably sting but I do what she says. It takes some effort but I finally get it in there and then she's maneuvering her legs so she's practically sitting on Brandon and then he's sliding up her cunt and my hands are finally on her breasts, the nipples tight and hard and Brandon is sucking on my knuckles or something and then I'm kissing Brandon and the sad cheerleader is laughing and shouting about how she's coming and then me and Brandon are both standing up, towering over her, jerking off, his cock huge, mine miniscule and then we're coming on the sad cheerleader and she's still laughing or maybe she's crying and I think it's a good thing we're in the bathtub.

She washes the come off and then Brandon asks if he could be alone for a few minutes so I leave the bathroom with Phone.

Buddy Becomes a Problem

Phone sits on the side of the bed. Buddy is on the other side, unconscious and lying in a pool of blood. The smell of rot fills the room and I open all the windows before going to the closet to get a clean t-shirt and pair of jeans. I can't find any jeans so I opt for sweat pants that have come stains in the crotch area from my strip club phase. Phone is still naked. She crosses her legs and says, "I'm worried about Buddy."

"Me too." I don't really know if this is true. I just decided Buddy was my best friend like three days ago and we haven't really had much of a conversation since then. I doubt he's even read *Dick Swap*. But this is a decision I had made and I have to follow it through to the end. "Also, would you mind if I put my mouth on your vagina?" I get down on my knees in front of her.

"I don't care." She spreads her legs. I start tonguing her vagina. It tastes nice. "We should probably take him to the hospital or something."

I pull my head back and say, "He'll probably be okay."

Phone rolls her eyes. "He's been leaking blood for at least two days. That's not normal. Even if he is Swedish or something."

My thirst quenched, I stand back up. "Thanks for letting me do that. It was nice. I've been wanting to since I first saw you but you always looked so dirty I thought it would be really gross. Buddy's Swedish?"

"He has *some* kind of accent."

"I say give it three days."

"He's been unconscious for a while. He's barely breathing. It looks like he's taken all of his pills. Maybe he's overdosed."

"We could call an ambulance. That would be a lot easier than taking him to the hospital."

"My phone doesn't work."

"Mine doesn't either."

"Maybe Brandon has a phone."

"Probably. He's looking really European, don't you think?"

"I don't even know what the hell that means."

"I'm sorry I'm slightly overweight and my penis is so small."

"What does that have to do with anything? Everything isn't about you."

But it is, I think. I'm all I've got. This would take too long to explain and just as I'm getting ready to say something, anything to break the silence, Brandon comes out of the bathroom dragging a fecal stench with him. He's wearing a t-shirt that says UNCLEAR and I try to remember if it was the same one he was wearing earlier. I squint my eyes to do this.

"What's up?" he asks, flipping his hair back with a toss of his head. He's definitely wearing the same pants. So European.

"We're thinking about taking Buddy to the hospital."

"Who's Buddy?"

I point to Buddy.

"Oh. He looks bad off."

"It would actually be a lot easier if we could just call an ambulance so we didn't have to try to lift him or move or exert ourselves too much."

"Yeah, I can totally dig that." He reaches into a pocket of his exotic jeans and pulls out a package of bacon. He pulls a piece of bacon from it, takes a lighter from the same pocket, and holds it under the bacon to warm it. "You don't even need to refrigerate this shit anymore."

I'm really hungry. Probably from all the vomiting I did this morning. Maybe I could grab something to eat on the way to the hospital. "Do you happen to have a phone?"

"I have one but it doesn't work."

"So I guess we're taking him to the hospital," I say.

"I need to get some clothes on," Phone says. She stands up and reaches between the mattress and the box springs. Brandon and I both stare at her ass while she does this. Brandon offers me the last bite of his bacon and I take it. Phone pulls out a cheerleader outfit identical to the one she discarded in the bathroom, only cleaner, and dresses.

"That guy's not wearing any pants and he's covered in blood," Brandon says. "Are we going to take him to the hospital like that?"

"I'll find something."

I rummage in the closet until I come up with a pair of jeans. They might be Agatha's. They look really small. I could have taken off my sweat pants and given them to him, but I didn't want to have to cram myself into Agatha's pants. I toss the pants to Phone. She begins pulling them onto Buddy before beckoning for help. I wait for Brandon to do it but he says, "Fuck man, I'm going to see if I can find some water or something."

So I help. "Maybe we should have cleaned him off first."

"No, this is better," Phone says.

After what feels like an hour, we finally get the jeans on him.

"I'm not going to be able to carry him down the stairs," I say.

"Why not? I'll help."

"I think I have spina bifida or something."

"That's stupid. I don't think that's what you think it is."

"Well, okay then, I'm just really tired."

"Lazy you mean."

"Let's just toss him out the window."

"That could kill him."

"He's almost dead anyway. Each second we spend debating it brings him even closer to death. You can't get him down the stairs by yourself. Unless you're planning on rolling him. If we toss him out the window, there's only one impact. If you roll him down the stairs he's getting ... impacted ... a lot more."

"You're an idiot."

"We can throw the mattress out first and then you can go down and break the fall. I'll drag him to the window but no further."

She throws her hands up like she's resigned. Like she doesn't have a choice. And she doesn't.

"Hey!" Brandon shouts up from downstairs. "I found some water!" He sounds victorious.

Throwing Buddy Out the Window

We roll Buddy onto the floor. He feels and sounds much like a wet towel. He smells like a bunch of rotting fruit, wrapped in a bunch of rotting meat, and then left to rot further in a rotting asshole. With a great deal of effort, we manage to cram the mattress through the window. At this point, I'm thinking it would have been easier just to roll him down the stairs. Phone goes downstairs and outside to break the fall. I try to lift Buddy. While he isn't as heavy as I thought he would be, I still can't lift him to the window. I shout for Brandon. It seems like he's been gone a really long time. I try to hold Buddy under the arms but I get tired and have to put him down. I look out the window. Phone is arranging the mattress. A group of maybe ten feral, hungry looking children is on the sidewalk, staring at Phone, waiting for her to bend down, hoping to get a glimpse of her underwear but, hell, just the sight of her in that outfit is enough to captivate them and I kind of empathize. Once the mattress is arranged she looks up. I wave to her. She shrugs her shoulders like, "So where's Buddy?" I give her a thumb up and disappear back into the room.

Brandon finally appears. He's drinking beer from a can. I didn't think there was any more beer left in the house.

"Where did you get the beer?"

"It's not beer. I filled it with water. All of your cups were dirty and I couldn't wash them out because the water didn't work even though we just took a bath and I managed to fill this can with water."

"How did you fill that can with water?"

"I used the hose."

"So maybe they only turned off some of the water."

"Whatever."

"Help me get Buddy out the window."

"That's a terrible idea."

"Why? Do you want to carry him down the stairs?"

"Look at him. If we throw him out the window he might explode."

"You don't even know him."

Brandon sighs and puts the can on the floor because the only surface in the room is the bed and the nightstand, which is covered with Buddy's empty pill bottles.

We manage to get Buddy up to the window and toss him out. I watch him fall. Phone isn't there to break the fall. She's cheering for the children or cheering for Buddy or cheering for something that I can't quite grasp. I can't really even grasp cheer. But Buddy hits the mattress okay and, at least from this distance, he doesn't appear to explode and looks basically exactly like he did before we threw him out the window. We go downstairs and I tell Brandon I have to check my MyFace page and my sales, the Fill the Grand Canyon fan page.

"Sales?"

"Yeah. For my book, *Dick Swap*."

"You wrote a book?"

"Yeah, there's a pile of them over there."

He dismissively waves his hand. "Nah, I don't read. Maybe if you could put it on a screen ..."

I flip open my laptop. I notice I have sold one copy of *Dick Swap* and my head goes wild. That's all it takes, I think. All it takes is the one right person buying it and then word of mouth will spread. What is one sale today could be two sales tomorrow and four sales the next day and so forth and so on. Exponential growth. The fucking snowball effect. I'm really an optimist.

Sadly, the Fill the Grand Canyon page is no longer on MyFace. There's an explanation of why they removed it in my email inbox. They said they took it down because it seemed like an act of terrorism. This is soul crushing. I want to explore it but I'm pressed for time. There are several other emails that appear to be MeTube links. I don't have time to watch any of them.

I look outside to see Brandon and Phone playing with the hose. They hold it up so the other one can drink from it. Then they spray Buddy with it. I guess Phone finally decided the blood covering Buddy was gross. They're smiling and laughing.

I go to my MyFace page and see that I have a friend request from Estelle. In the message section, it says:

MISS YOU HEAR IN JOLLY TOWN MY JOLLY JIBBLES ARE HARD AND HOT FOR YOU. YOU ARE THE ELECTRIC

MAESTRO. WE'LL GALLOP FORLORNLY.

Against my better judgment, I click accept and quickly close the laptop. Like even thinking about Estelle is going to carve something else onto my body. Maybe even onto my soul. And then I think I should have given her some sort of reply. Something like, "Thanks for the pentagram!" but it's too late now. We have to get Buddy to a hospital.

Outside and the day is crisp and blue. A number of black smoke plumes rise up from houses like tornadoes. For a second I forget where I am and what I'm doing. I think about collapsing onto the porch, curling into a fetal position and having a good cry. Then I remember Buddy and Phone and Brandon and realize this is the most company I've had since I met Agatha. Why didn't I check Agatha's MyFace page while I was in there?

I cross to the side of the house but Phone and Brandon are already walking Buddy to the car. Maybe it's good someone has stolen the passenger seat. I open the passenger side door, remove a feral child who's sitting in the back seat eating meat from something resembling a human femur, and Brandon and Phone place Buddy's torso on the floor and prop his legs up on the back seat. They both get in the rear passenger door, Phone on Brandon's lap, and we're on our way to the hospital, Brandon fingering Phone the entire time.

Let's All Go to the Hospital

I'm so into watching what's going on in the backseat I almost forget where I'm going. Not that I really knew anyway. I could never afford to go to the hospital and had never been there. I'm pretty sure Dayton has a hospital. Maybe more than one. My plan is to drive until I begin seeing the blue and white hospital signs. Or until I find an ambulance with its sirens on. In the backseat, they just keep going and going. I wonder if it's the hash. They both acted mostly unaffected back at the house. Maybe they've taken something else. God only knows what Brandon has in those pants. I remember how hungry I am and drive through a McDonald's. I don't bother asking Brandon or Phone if they want anything because they seem preoccupied and, to be honest, I'm just a little jealous. Estelle was merely a stand in for Agatha. Agatha was very attractive. Phone is also very attractive. Even more so when she's not covered in a layer of grime. But I'm even able to overlook the grime. It's the shape that really counts. The visual outlines and how she feels beneath my hands. She does seem a little on the mean and impatient side, at least with me, but Agatha was mostly abusive. I order chicken nuggets and fries. I refuse to call them McNuggets and the speaker person seems confused, possibly even angry, insistently reading the order back to me as "Chicken McNuggets". I also get a really big Coke in the hopes that the Monopoly game is still going on. The big Coke yields two chances to win. I need all the chances I can get. I will be able to eat this food in the car on the way to the hospital without making too big of a mess. McDonald's true selling point. Not that it really matters.

I finish the box of nuggets and toss it out the window. I slurp my Coke, belch, and see the first sign for the hospital. The sky is darkening. I wonder how long I've been driving around. How long

Brandon has had various parts of his body in Phone's vagina. I can't seem to quit thinking about Phone's vagina. A car's following us with its lights turned on super bright. I continue following directions to the hospital. The car keeps following us.

The hospital is packed. It's like a giant party. I park in front of the emergency room doors. In India beggars maim themselves so they can elicit more pity from their potential contributors. In Dayton people lightly injure themselves so they can get more pain medicine to either sell or take as recreational drugs. It's cheaper than any of the street stuff you can buy. Especially if you have insurance or Medicare. I wonder what the hell's wrong with Buddy. I hope they don't think he's faking it just to get stop bleeding medication. That can't be normal. Although, now that Phone and Brandon have taken it upon themselves to hose him off before putting him in the car, I hope he's actually bleeding when the doctor sees him.

I get out of the car after Phone and Brandon. I don't want them to think I'm the one handling this just because I drove. If anyone should handle it, it should be Phone. Brandon goes just inside the first door and grabs a wheelchair. The car following us is still behind me. Idling. No one has gotten out. I glance up and catch Estelle's ghoulish unwigged head through the windshield. I instinctively grab the top of my head to make sure I'm not still wearing the wig. I'm not sure when I lost it. Maybe she took it back after carving the pentagram in my chest. Maybe that's why she carved the pentagram in my chest. But if she'd taken it back she'd be wearing it now. She lays on the horn. I ignore her and help Brandon and Phone load Buddy into the wheelchair. Luckily, he'd worked up a pretty good blood in all the driving around. Phone sits on his lap to keep him upright in the chair and Brandon pushes them into the hospital. Now I feel vaguely useless. I could move the car but that would mean navigating it into the parking garage and Estelle would surely follow me. She'd probably try to hurt me. I wish Chuck Barrymore inhabited this garage. He'd help me out. Chuck would do anything for me, I'm sure. Like that time he let me use his phone...

I follow them in. The waiting room is full of people, prescription drug addicts slumped in chairs and their significant others there to enable them. I tell Buddy and Phone I'll get us all checked in, even though I have no idea how it works. I always assumed a trip to the hospital would be like a million dollars so I typically just wait for things to clear up in a few days. Mostly it seems to have worked. It's forced me to lead a life of caution.

I wander up to one of the hospital cashiers. She stares vacantly and fatly at me.

"Buddy's bleeding," I say.

"You'll need to fill this out." She slides several sheets of paper in a clipboard to me. I fill out the forms to the best of my ability. Since I don't know a lot about Buddy, it's mostly blank or made up.

She looks at the form and her eyes get normal, as wide as they can possibly get.

"What's his last name?"

I turn around. Phone still sits on Buddy's lap. Brandon sits on the floor next to the wheelchair. "Hey, what's Buddy's last name!" I shout. Since Phone has a thing with him, I think she might know.

"Is that his wife?" the cashier asks.

"In some countries," I say.

"What's her last name?"

"Pointless."

"And who are you?"

"Andy Boring. I'm his nephew."

"And he doesn't have insurance?"

"He might."

She huffs out an exasperated sigh. "You make my vagina itch. And not in a good way. A yeasty way."

"What do we do now?"

"Sit and wait like everybody else."

"But they're all drug addicts. Look at them. This is like party central. Buddy's covered in blood. We don't even know where it's coming from. He's been like that for days. His mouth is covered in sores. His mustache is limp and listless."

"I don't think he'll be dying anytime soon."

"You know nothing," I hiss before walking back to join the rest.

"What now?" Phone asks.

"We wait."

"Fucking bullshit."

Brandon stands up, probably aided by his fabulous foreign-as-fuck pants, and says, "I'm going to go out to the car and get high."

"I'm going to go with him," Phone says.

"I'll wait here with Buddy." This isn't what I want to do at all. Phone and Brandon are going to go out to the car and smoke hash and then they're going to have sex. I want to go out there with them but feel like staying with Buddy is the responsible thing to do or maybe I'm slightly mad at Phone because I thought we would be having more sex than we are even though we haven't really come to any sort of arrangement.

They turn to leave and a man who looks like a porn star enters wearing a t-shirt that says, in furry hot pink lettering: SEX WRANGLER.

All the chairs are full so I sit on Buddy's lap.

Sex Wrangler goes to the line of cashier nurses and I notice he has a large dildo in each of his back pockets.

We wait for hours. I'm pretty sure Buddy stops breathing two or three times. Brandon and Phone never come back. I really thought Phone was more responsible than this. But I guess you should never trust a girl in a cheerleading uniform. I tell myself it's just taking them this long because they've already had so much sex that it's probably taking Brandon a really long time to come.

Eventually we're called and I wheel Buddy back to a curtained off area. The doctor comes in. He seems really rushed. His nametag says, "Dr. Blast."

"Bleeding?" He looks up from his chart.

"Yes."

"From where?"

"All over. Maybe his pores, then?"

"We'll need to get those clothes off and take some x-rays."

The doctor helps me strip Buddy down. He looks like a corpse. He's very thin and blood is bubbling and crusting over his skin. The doctor does something fancy to the gurney and wheels it through the curtains. There's a TV in the room. It's mounted on the only real wall, which is above where the patient's head would rest when the hospital bed was in there. It didn't make a lot of sense. Maybe it was so the person here with the patient could stare at both the patient and the TV.

I flip it on. It's *Dan Banal* and I get really excited. I think this is the one where Dan drinks a cup of coffee and eats a piece of toast.

He's talking into his cell phone. "Okay, honey, I'm going to put you on speaker phone."

"Why?" It's his wife.

"So I can pour myself a cup of coffee and make some toast."

Fill the Grand Canyon and Live Forever

Dan pulls a stainless steel carafe from a modern looking coffee maker. He pours it into a cup sitting on the counter.

"I just poured the coffee."

"Great job." There isn't a trace of sarcasm in his wife's voice.

He pulls a toaster out from a kitchen cabinet, sits it on the counter, and plugs it into the wall. He goes to another cabinet and pulls out a loaf of bread. He removes the plastic tab that holds the bag closed. He extracts one piece of bread and puts it in the toaster. He twists the top of the bread bag and puts the plastic tab back on it. Then he depresses the lever on the toaster, picks up his coffee cup, and takes a sip. He picks up his phone and says, "Okay, it's toasting."

Dan Banal fades and is replaced by a swooping shot of the Grand Canyon. Instant vertigo. Hate and fear. The words "Life Forever" scroll across. An emaciated old man wanders into camera range. He has dark circles under his eyes and looks near death. It's almost like he's hovering above the Grand Canyon. Staring at him floating there makes me almost nauseous. What channel is this? I try to change it but nothing happens. I collapse into a chair, stare at the TV, unable to look away, paralyzed by fear.

"Let the pilgrimage begin," the man says. The audio is bad. Ripples of static occasionally flicker across the screen like it's being broadcast from someplace very away. Farther even than the Grand Canyon. I don't even know what state the Grand Canyon is in. "I had a vision. I was lying in my deathbed, disease had eaten my brain, and I had a vision. We are the garbage people. We are the saviors. I had a vision. Lying on the brink of death in life, standing at the edge of the Grand Canyon in my vision. I look down. I had super strong steroid eyes of strength. I could see all the way to the bottom of that canyon and what I saw was a pit of despair. A pit of lies. A pit of longing and unfulfilled dreams. A pit of death. Do you want to know where the Devil comes from? The very bottom, the very depths of the Grand Canyon. Because the Devil is real and the Devil exists and the Devil is disease and the Devil and all his minions must be destroyed. We will conquer. We come from the stars. Just like Evil Knievel. We have sparks for eyes. Why must our national parks be kept pristine? Do you know why? I'll tell you why. So the rich have somewhere to hide when the revolution comes. You want to know what they're doing to our national parks at this point? Building fences around them. Putting up armed guards. Securing their post-Empire plots of land. And what are they building around everyone else? Landfills. Trash palaces. They own the corporations that sell you this junk so you can one day die surrounded by your life of consumption. But you can only take advantage of the star people for so long before we become monsters. We will fight back with our snack food wrappers, junked cars, used condoms, and spent cigarette butts. We will rise up and strip the rich of their strongholds. We will find the Devil in his lair and smother him with his own poison! We will fill the Grand Canyon and live forever!"

At this point, the words, correct now, "Live Forever" float across the screen and the old man just stands there looking tired and creepy and staring into the camera. The screen goes black and there's a name, "Eldon Muntz", followed by a PO Box that looks like maybe it's on another planet. I try to digest what just went on. Thinking back on it, the old man probably only spoke for about thirty seconds but it felt like much longer than that. It seemed like he wanted viewers to do something but I wasn't exactly sure. It seems like he was sick and now he was, well, at least not dead. I kind of want him to come back on. Minus the religious stuff, I think our ideas our similar.

A newscast pops up and the anchorman says, "Why are people flocking to the Grand Canyon—"

The doctor pushes Buddy into the room.

I stand up.

Phone enters, panting, smelling heavily of sex and hash. Maybe a little like ass, which could fall under sex, I guess. I bet Brandon fisted her. Fabulously fisted her. Thinking about it arouses me. I wonder how far he got his arm up there. He probably had to stay in the car and rest up. I think about moving close enough to Phone to press my erection against her.

Phone touches me on the elbow. "We need to talk."

Before I can ask her what about, the doctor says, "I've got odd news."

"Odd how?"

"Well, he's still alive. That's good, I guess. But take a look at these x-rays ..." He pulls the x-rays out of a folder and clips them to a lighted board. I don't really see anything resembling the human anatomy on there.

"I'm not sure I understand."

"Exactly. It's all black. I've never seen an x-ray quite like this. Are you sure your friend is human?"

"I ..." I'd never really thought about it. If he were some kind of space creature, that would explain a lot.

"Andy?" Phone taps my elbow again. Listening to the doctor seems pretty important. I can't really imagine something more important than learning that Buddy is all black inside, possibly not even human. I think about asking if I can get my brain examined while I'm there. That seems pretty important too. Ever since having the Grand Canyon fan page revoked it's felt like the cracks and holes are spreading at an alarming rate. What shred of rational thought I had left might soon leave.

Phone smacks me gently on the cheek. Maybe not so gently.

"What?" I feel irritable.

"Who's Estelle?"

Oh shit. I turn my attention back to the doctor and wonder how I became the person in charge of this whole Buddy situation. But I'm a doer. The fact of the Fill the Grand Canyon fan page being removed is a sign of that. Me as instigator. I still had plans and wasn't sure anything needed to change. "Okay, well, can we wrap this up so we can get Buddy home?"

"We don't have a car," Phone says.

I'm pretty sure we used to have a car. Pretty sure that's how we got here.

The doctor says, "I'll write out some prescriptions and he'll need to rest. If he dies, I'd probably burn him and make sure not to breathe in any of the fumes. Not sure if whatever he has is contagious or not. As I said before, I'm at a loss." Doctor Blast threw up his thick hands, the motion causing his white lab coat to pull back and I'm able to read his t-shirt for the fist time:

WORST DOCTOR EVER

"Can you prescribe a car or some mode of transportation, also?" Phone asks.

The doctor looks at her and blinks slowly. "The parking garage is full of those. In fact, I'll help you find one. I'm about off duty anyway."

A Swift Punch to the Dick Solves Nothing

We can't find Buddy's clothes so we drag him back into the wheelchair and Phone sits on his lap. The doctor hands us a sheaf of prescriptions and I roll Buddy and Phone out to the lobby. It's still like a party, complete with loud classic rock music and topless haggard beasts. We've been there so long, I'm assuming many of these people have been there, gotten their prescriptions filled, and returned for more. There's never last call at a hospital. The party goes on all night.

I wheel Buddy and phone out by the curb. It feels warmer than I think it should be. I realize I have no idea what month it is. I still think I'm coming down with some kind of brain disorder. Not surprisingly, the car isn't out here. I begin wheeling us toward the parking garage. Doctor Blast shuffles along behind us.

I think about asking Phone what happened but it doesn't matter. Whatever happened happened. Now the important thing is that we don't have a car and Brandon seems to be missing.

Phone volunteers the information anyway. She also has questions.

"That Estelle bitch is crazy. Who is she?"

"Just a fling."

"She seems a little old."

"She's a lot old."

"She kidnapped Brandon."

"I'm glad he came back. I hadn't seen him in a very long time. I was hoping he would be here longer. But ... those pants. Do you think him and Buddy got along?"

"Well I don't really think it was his choice to get abducted. Should we try to find him?"

"We probably could. But that would mean finding Estelle, too. I don't really want to do that."

"What if something happens to him?"

"He's an adult. He can take of himself, I'm sure. Estelle's mostly harmless." I remember the pentagram carved onto my chest, the person dissolved in her kitchen sink, the dealing drugs to school children, the hit and runs, the house fires ... Estelle is actually, to this point, the most dangerous person I know. But I decide not to tell Phone any of this.

"Are you involved in something bad?"

"Not at all. I'm just a guy who gets up and goes to work and comes home and hangs out with his best bud." I grab Buddy's gummy shoulder and give it a shake. "Do you know how to hotwire a car?"

"Of course."

"We're going to need to do that."

I wheel us up to a modest car. Phone's still sitting on Buddy's lap. I cross over to the side of the wheelchair, tug down my pants, and pull out my penis.

"What am I supposed to do with that?"

"Suck it. I've been thinking about fucking you since you went outside with Brandon."

"Why don't you fuck me then? No one will see." Doctor Blast is wandering around the bright garage, tugging on door handles. I think Phone underestimates his ability to turn around.

"Nah. Now your vagina's full of come. I'd rather have a blowjob."

She reaches out and grabs my penis, leans into it. It doesn't take long for me to come. She swallows it all. She wipes off her bottom lip and I punch her in the forehead. I have no idea why and apologize immediately. She punches me in the dick and it hurts quite a bit. I bend over and vomit while she busts out the window to the car and hotwires it.

Doctor Blast wanders over and says, "They're all locked."

I tell him we live in a dangerous world and wonder how many knife wounds, gunshots, and blunt head trauma victims he's treated in the emergency room. I think about giving him a hug.

I throw Buddy into the back seat and we leave the parking garage, heading for the all night drugstore.

Blast's phone must vibrate or something because he pulls it out of his pocket and says, "Hello."

The polite thing to do would be to not listen but I can't help it.

"Oh, hi, Hansel."

"..." I wish he would put him on speaker phone.

"I agree. That is very ambiguous."

"…"

"It's been a year? Why didn't you call me sooner?"

"…"

"I see."

"…"

"I have your number now. I can call back and we can resume treatment. I'm a little tied up at the moment."

"…"

"Goodbye."

"Can you get the Internet on that thing?"

"I once encouraged a man to jump out of a window. It's taken him this long to hit the ground. I can get just about anything."

We leave Buddy in the car to go into the drugstore. The lights are harsh and bright. It has that smell universal to every drugstore everywhere. Something like rubber, plastic, and air conditioning. Sterile, but cloyingly so. Phone goes to the back to drop off the prescriptions. I wander into the candy aisle and start eating candy bars. I get really thirsty. I find a cooler and drink one of those little plastic bottles of chocolate milk. I can't remember the last time I had a craving for milk. I see Candy from the elevator factory. She's buying a lot of make-up and weight loss products. I drift into another aisle and hide. I don't want her to see me. I'm pretty sure I've missed a day or two of work without calling or anything. I've probably been fired. If I had a phone for them to call, they probably would have let me know this. Phone finds me. She's carrying a shopping bag full of pills and ointments. We hurry back outside.

There's a big red Cadillac parked beside our stolen car. A charred corpse is strapped to the top of it. I have a feeling Estelle might be behind the wheel.

Phone crosses to the driver side. I make for the passenger side. I don't want to look inside the Cadillac but I do anyway. Estelle is sitting in the driver's seat, smoking. She has a different wig on and I think maybe she's trying to disguise herself. This one is long and flowing, like maybe it's trying to represent ringlets but it's kind of old and ratty and matted. A very young girl is sitting in the passenger seat and looking terrified.

"Where ya going, Porky?" Estelle hisses out the window.

"I don't know what you want from me, Estelle."

"I want a good time. Just like any girl."

"I have a different girl now."

I look to Phone for support but she just shakes her head.

"You looking for Agatha? Is that where you're going?"

"No. Fuck Agatha. She's dead to me."

"How do you like what I done with your friend?" She stabs her cigarette toward the roof. "He sure had some cock on him. Nowhere near as small as yours."

I hurry into the car and tell Phone we need to go. No amount of talking to Estelle is going to make her seem less crazy. I know she'll follow us, but at least we'll be moving. Phone backs up and powers the car onto the road.

"Where to?" she asks.

"The Grand Canyon!" I yell, happy to be moving, happy to be getting away from Estelle, charging toward something that might prove to be eternal life.

Doctor Blast is staring into his phone. "You don't mind if I ride along with you guys, do you?"

"We might be gone a while," I say.

"That's okay. I don't really have any plans or anything."

"Can I borrow your phone?"

"Can I come with you?"

"*Yes.* Can I borrow your phone? And can you look inside my head and tell me what's wrong with me?"

He hands me his phone. "I don't really need to look into your head. I can tell from the outside."

"And ..."

"Give me a while."

"That's a frustrating answer."

"Would you rather I lie?"

I have to think about this. I stop thinking about it.

"What the fuck?" Phone asks. "The Grand Canyon?"

I take a really long time to explain the infomercial or whatever it was to her. She doesn't seem to exactly understand but is happy for what sounds like a vacation. I tell her to pay attention. Now I'm looking at Blast's phone, checking MyFace to make sure the Grand Canyon fan page hasn't miraculously returned. I check my email that is even more filled with links to MeTube videos. I click on the first link. It's a newscast about the traffic around the Grand Canyon. The newscaster compares to a hajj, whatever that is. There's another news story about a man arrested for emptying a dump truck into the Grand Canyon. A later news story that includes an interview with a family who had loaded their RV with all of their belongings and drove it to the Canyon to throw everything in but they were stopped. The interviewer asks the husband why he would want to do that and he says, "It seemed like a good idea." And there are more videos. Many more. Most of these are of lower quality, recorded on people's phones. Some of the scenes were filmed at night. Others were shot in broad daylight. People were recording themselves throwing an assortment of items into the Canyon. Some of them even pissing and shitting into it. And while all of this amazes me, I'm even more taken by what is happening in the background of these recordings. The sheer volume of trash in the Canyon and the amount of vehicles surrounding it. Not just civilian vehicles but also things that look like military vehicles. The last one I'm able to watch is of a man wearing an orange jumpsuit, accused of throwing over a hundred people in the Canyon in the last few days. When asked why he did it, he says, "I want everyone to live forever."

I don't know how to feel about this.

A Cross-country Hunter S. Thompsonish Adventure in 574 Words

And our road trip is underway. It will really only take a little over a day to get to the Grand Canyon if we drive round the clock. But we feel like making it take longer. Given that the Grand Canyon brought Eldon Muntz back from the brink of death, we don't feel extremely pressed for time in regards to Buddy. He'll either die or he won't. We give him some of his prescriptions but Phone and I split most of them. And Doctor Blast is there so we can always get more if we need them. Estelle and her teenager follow us the entire time. We're stopped by the police a few times and manage to wit our way out of each situation. A Kansas State Trooper mentions something about the car being stolen and Phone ends up giving him a blow job beside his cruiser. It's pretty late at night. I think the trooper is drunk. It's difficult driving under the influence of all the pills, but we manage to do it. And, if ever Phone and I are both incapacitated, Doctor Blast takes the wheel like a seasoned pro. Occasionally we stop off in cheap hotels or rest stops and have mind blowing sex. We try to involve Buddy a couple of times but once he vomits and once he comes blood so it isn't a lot of fun. Doctor Blast never joins in. He says sex is a destructive force. He has weird theories. We monitor the Grand Canyon situation and it continues to "escalate". That's how all the news footage puts it. I begin to fear or possibly hope that I'm somehow complicit in instigating this but so many people come forward to say it was their idea I feel either let down or off the hook. The car breaks down a couple of times and we find ways to make it work, realizing there isn't anything we don't have at our disposal: Phone's sexual wiles, Buddy's condition, drugs, my borderline retardation, Doctor Blast's big doctory brain.

A few hours from the Grand Canyon Phone falls asleep and I turn on the radio. It sounds like static and wind. Then a voice says, "Ahhh, that's the sound of the Grand Canyon." Then there's a sound like a truck backing up and a bunch of clinking and rattling. "And that's the sound of the Grand Canyon being filled with trash. Don't let this happen to our national parks. Donate to the National Park Foundation." This is followed by the sound of machine gun fire and a different voice rattling off a website, a Twitter account, a MyFace location, a Tumblr account, a MeTube station, and a number of blogs.

I turn the radio off and try not to show any fear.

As we get closer to the Canyon, the traffic becomes increasingly bumper to bumper. Huge vehicles laden with trash. Small vehicles stuffed, their doors and trunks open to accommodate more. Some even have trash bags strapped to the top of the car. It's like a moving landfill. Buddy's looking really bad. Doctor Blast hasn't been the greatest help in the world and I'm starting to feel concerned. Doctor Blast leans his head out the window and makes a braying siren noise. This does nothing to help so Phone swerves the car onto the shoulder and we continue our drive to the Canyon. Blast continues to make the siren noises.

Phone Just Isn't the Same

It's almost three in the morning by the time we get there. A few guard posts cross the streets and the arms are down, barring our entrance. I sit before the one in the middle, the car idling, and think about what Muntz said in his infomercial or call to arms. He was right. The Grand Canyon is being protected from the common man. There are probably whole gaggles of rich people in there, drinking champagne, playing golf, having sex with children, whatever it is really rich people do. Even though I haven't paid taxes in a number of years, I feel offended that I'm being kept from something my tax dollars would have theoretically helped pay for. I don't not pay taxes for any political reasons. It's just too difficult to figure out.

As if to reaffirm this opinion, I'm staring at a handpainted sign that reads: NATIONAL PARK MY ASS. THIS IS A GATED COMUNITTY!!!

"Ready?" I ask Phone but she's either asleep or unconscious from all of Buddy's prescriptions she's consumed. I back up so I can get a good start and slam into the gate. We should have stolen a better car. The gate folds the hood of the car into itself and smashes the windshield.

Phone lurches in her seat and says, "What the fuck?"

"I had to crash through the gate."

The road trip has changed Phone. Whereas I am exactly the same person I was when we began, only maybe a little more relaxed without all of those things at home to deal with, Phone has become wired and anxious. Maybe it's all the drugs, the lack of food, or the call to sex in wildly uncomfortable places and circumstances, but she isn't the same person she was when we started. At a truck stop in Texas, she was trying to cheer for a lot lizard giving a blowjob to a trucker and, midway through, became too depressed to continue. I hope the lot lizard managed to finish the blowjob. She certainly looked like she could have used some encouragement.

I place a hand on her thigh. It's meant to be comforting but it's really more lecherous than anything. "Are you worried about Buddy?"

"Who?"

"Buddy." I jerk my head toward the back seat. Briefly panicked that we'd left him at one of the hotels, I turn my head to make sure he's still back there.

"Whatever," Phone says. "What are we supposed to do with him?"

"I'm not exactly sure but it has something to do with the Grand Canyon."

"What are we going to do? Throw him in there?"

"Maybe ..." I hadn't really considered it.

"That probably will not work," Blast volunteers.

I'd forgotten he was back there and his voice startles me. "Have you figured out what's wrong with me yet? You've had like three days."

"You have no sense of purpose. No sense of self-worth. No ... narrative."

"No narrative?"

"None at all."

"I don't even know what you mean."

"Everybody else around you has one. You don't. You're just existing in other people's lives. Without them ..."

"Ominous." I meet his eyes in the rearview mirror.

"Embrace it."

"What about my brain tumor?"

"You probably don't have one. I've seen you operate a motor vehicle."

"And that's how they diagnose those things?"

"It's how I diagnose those things."

"Are you a brain doctor?"

"I'm a life doctor. I can take care of anything."

"Confident."

I pull into a parking lot and see a number of lights in the near distance. I wonder if these are the aliens Muntz was talking about. Already his speechy infomercial has become jumbled in my head. I'm not sure if he was saying he was an alien or the rich people he was battling were aliens or what. I decide to drive toward the lights, careful not to plummet into the Canyon itself.

There are also lights behind us. That's probably Estelle. She's followed us the entire way but hasn't done anything too crazy. At least not to us. Maybe she's on the run. Maybe someone back in Ohio figured out what she was into. I wasn't even sure of the extent of her madness but I know most of what she did was illegal. We're probably going to have some kind of showdown. I'm not really sure what she wants from me. I'm not going to become one of her white slaves or whatever it is she wants. I can't imagine anyone having any interest in a portly middle-aged guy as a white slave anyway. Maybe she just wants to use me as a sacrifice. I don't really have much of an interest in that, either.

After rolling a little farther, I'm able to tell the lights in front of us belong to trucks. Large dump trucks backed up to the Grand Canyon, filling it with trash. Fuck yes, I think. These people have the right idea. They'll know what to do with Buddy.

Before getting out of the car, I remember the weird dream I had about the Grand Canyon. The charred corpse of one person in that dream is strapped to Estelle's car. No one has heard from the other one since going to the Grand Canyon. And I'm at the Grand Canyon now, only feet away from the precipice, the beckoning abyss, for the first time since my honeymoon and the beginning of the end of my marriage. I wonder if I have a fear of heights or a fear of suicide. I don't seem to get as anxious, nauseous and weak kneed if I'm somehow restrained, like on a roller coaster or something. Maybe it's all the drugs or the driving or the sleep deprivation or just being around Phone who's become like a robotic walking corpse or maybe it's whatever I have living inside my head or whatever is missing from my head, but I feel really strange and disoriented.

I stumble out of the car.

A flabby man stands beside one of the dump trucks. He's holding a rake and sticking it into the inclined bed of the truck and raking the trash out. It flutters into the Canyon, down into the darkness. The man is standing so close. I have to stay on the other side of the car. I can feel the Canyon pulling at me. It wants to consume me. Not that it really matters. I could dive into the Canyon and no one would really miss me. I think Agatha may have loved me at one point but we'd both gotten weird. And then she left with all those coats. I wasn't sure if I could forgive her for that. Buddy is my best friend but it looks like he's going to die. Phone? I'm pretty sure it's just physical between us. And a pretty lame kind of physical. Mainly I'm just really mean to her and put my penis in certain parts of her anatomy when I feel like it. I seem to have even stolen the cheer from her. Estelle's crazy. And homicidal. And old.

And while the physical canyon yawns before me, I can feel the cracks and the holes in my head open farther, trying to drink whatever I have left. Do I *have* anything left? I've told myself I feel good, told myself I was having fun, told myself a lot of things. Even told myself I've felt things. But what I really feel is empty. Other people's emotions are my emotions. I try to feel what they're feeling. Try to feel something but sometimes I think if I was all alone and in a quiet place, I'd hear the wind rushing between the empty walls of my brain.

I brace myself against the trunk. It feels like everything is moving too fast and too slow at the same time. Like someone has rapidly wiped their thumb across a picture, smudging it, leaving me standing in some type of blurred landscape.

Estelle hops up on the top of her car, naked and straddling Brandon's corpse. She shouts, "I've never felt this alive!"

But I feel near death. That's how opposite Estelle and I are.

Phone steps out of the car, collapses to her knees, and vomits.

The man who is raking trash moves over to her and says, "You don't waste that. Move over there to the ledge." Phone, ever obedient, scoots to the edge of the Canyon and vomits into it. The man with the rake tries to rake her previous puddle of puke over the ledge.

I stumble over to the man with the rake. "Hey, man, I'm a little out of it and I don't know what's going on. We've driven all the way from Ohio. Ohio! You know where that is? We don't have an ocean or a canyon or anything. Just shit. Anyway we've driven non-stop because I saw that thing about the pilgrimage on TV. I'm also the one who started an awesome MyFace page about filling this thing but I couldn't help out because I lived all the way in Ohio. We want to join up. That's why we drove all the way out here. From Ohio. Vomitland." I look at Phone, bent over and retching. "That's probably why she's like that. Ohio and all."

The man's just holding his rake and staring at me. I'm hoping he'll be a little more helpful.

"Anyway I'm kind of wondering what the fucking deal is. See, one of the reasons ... Okay the *only* reason we drove all the way here from Ohio was so that we could heal my bud Buddy. You want to take a look at him? He's really bad off. He's covered in blood and we were mostly too tired and lazy to wash the blood off him so he looks as bad as he probably feels and we took him to the hospital and the doctor said that his insides were all black and he wasn't really sure what that meant and then the doctor came with us but I don't see him anywhere. You don't think it's cancer, do you? And then the doctor gave us a whole bunch of pills but they didn't really seem to work and then I thought maybe Buddy's from space, maybe Buddy's like an alien or something ... What do you think? Do you know how we might be able to make him better? Do we have to wait until the Grand Canyon's full of trash or what?"

The man holds up a large callused hand. It's about the size of my face. "Please stop talking. I can only understand about half of what you're saying. I'll take a look at him."

"Aw jeez thanks."

Phone is still vomiting over the edge. Actually she doesn't really seem to be vomiting at the moment. Just slumped over and breathing heavily. Estelle is dousing her giant Cadillac in gas. I realize she's not completely naked. She's wearing cowboy boots and shouting, "Yee-haw," as she splashes the gas.

The man with the rake shuts the car door and says, "That guy's dead."

"What?"

"That guy's dead. He's probably been dead for a while."

"What should we do?" I laugh nervously. "Why didn't Doctor Blast tell us that?"

"Fuck if I know. Throw him over. We could use him."

"That's equating Buddy to trash. Buddy is not trash!"

Phone has wobbled back over to me. She flaps her hand at me and says, "Just do what he says. We've got other things to worry about."

"That's such a fucking shit solution!" I kick out but I don't know where I'm kicking and fall down on the ground. I imagine everyone is laughing at me with their smudge faces. Estelle's car goes up with a whoosh and I can smell gas and burning meat and realize how hungry I am. I don't want to just throw Buddy into the Canyon like a piece of trash but then Estelle's flaming car slams into our stolen car and they both go hurtling down into the Canyon. I manage to stand up and wander over to the edge with everybody else. I'm woozy and afraid of falling in but I don't care. The cars crash on protuberances on the way down and then burst into flame as they hit the bottom. The flame is huge, like a giant ball of light. I imagine part of the fire breaking off, rocketing up toward the top of the Canyon and then right in front of us. I tell myself it's Buddy as it continues shooting up into the star filled sky, growing smaller and smaller.

Buddy. Returning to space. Has to be.

Doctor Blast stands beside me, surveying the rims of the Canyon. It's hazy and blurry and dark but in the glow of so many headlights and floodlights and even searchlights from overhead, I can see there are people everywhere. "All of these people need helped," Doctor Blast says.

I want to ask him what about me, don't I need help? But he doesn't even acknowledge me as he goes walking off into the night.

Everything swims in front of me.

I can hear muffled laughter.

I back away from the Canyon before I fall in.

Nothing Can Be Fixed

The world is black and mean-spirited.

I'm going over the edge of the Grand Canyon at night. Weightless. Drifting slowly down. The water of a river twinkles below me. I spread my arms and my legs like I have a parachute attached to me but there isn't one. There is nothing to break my fall. I think of Brandon and Greg doing this so many years ago. I wonder if it helped them at all. I really wanted to find out more about Brandon's life while he was away. I really want to know what happened to Greg. What happened to me? What happens to anybody? Inky night is slipping past me, around me, and I'm wondering if this is going to be the end. Or is it going to be the beginning. Once out of high school, I can't recall being optimistic about anything. If it's the beginning of something then it's going to be something terrible. What do I have? Really? Nothing. There is nothing except what is in my head but I've been trying to distract myself from that. Agatha was the glue that held everything together. And maybe I didn't really like her very much. I think I should be gaining speed as I plummet farther but I maintain the same speed. Like a feather or something. Maybe this is only me exploring some kind of mystery. The mystery of what? The mystery of falling? The mystery of dying? That's not a mystery at all. You die and then you're dead. You're trash. Might as well end up at the bottom of the Grand Canyon anyway. What's the difference between being at the bottom of the Canyon and being buried under a few feet of polluted dirt? I can't see one. If there's a god he's a sick bastard. He's probably really good friends with Estelle. He probably smiles on people like Estelle.

Near the bottom, I see a shape on the bank of the river. As I drift farther and farther, the shape becomes more apparent. It's Agatha.

She's added even more coats. She's huge. It's like she's spent the last week or so wandering across the country and adding coats. I land on her and she breaks my fall. I roll off.

"That's ... a lot of coats," I say. "Why did you leave like that?"

"I felt cold. I went to find more coats."

"Are you warm?"

"No. I'm dead inside."

"Things have gotten really bad since you left."

"Things were always bad."

"Were they? I don't think they were. I think things were just normal."

"Things were terrible. We're *both* dead inside."

"I don't think that's true. I feel pretty good inside. It seems like everything that's outside is shit. And I think you just want more than you can possibly have. You can never have everything."

"You're brain damaged."

"Why do you say that?"

"It's like all your fat went into your brain and stopped it from working. Come on, *Dick Swap*? Who's going to buy that shit?"

"At least I wasn't sleeping around."

"I wasn't either."

"Oh, come on ... Buddy?"

"Buddy just showed up one day. I was waiting for you to ask him to leave. When you didn't, I decided I would."

"But he missed you. He said your name."

"That doesn't mean we were fucking. How's that stupid cheerleader working out for you anyway?"

"She's pretty attractive. And she gives a really good blowjob and doesn't mind it when I fuck her in the ass but I'm not really anything special to her. Just a man and a dick to fill her when she needs it, which is like all the time. I've also had sex with Estelle, a really old sociopath."

"So I guess you've gotten over me."

"I was pretty upset when you left but I haven't had a whole lot of time to think about it. Like I said, things got really crazy. They went really bad."

"And you think me coming back would fix that?"

I think about that for a second. I'm not even sure there's any place to go back to. "No," I say. "Nothing can be fixed."

"Good. Because I'm never coming back."

I hear a sound from above. When I lift my head to look, I'm covered by a bunch of trash, stinking and suffocating.

"You're doing it wrong."

I'm not sure whose voice that is.

"Stop fucking criticizing me. I know more than you." I know who that is. That's Estelle.

"Dammit, Estelle. Did you hit him with the shovel first?"

Phone? It might be Phone.

"I did, honey, but I ain't as strong as I used to be."

"And what did you do with Chloe? If she runs off she could blow everything."

"You need to stop with your shit mouth. I've been doing this for a long time. Chloe's handcuffed to the steering wheel. And even if she wasn't she wouldn't run off and blab. She's been through the program. Just like all the girls at home. They're loyal only to us."

"I'm sorry. I don't know where my head is. It's been a rough week."

Another clump of something hits me in the face.

"Please don't bury me alive!" I shout. I try to kick out but they clearly foresaw this and have bound my arms and legs. Shouting has filled my mouth with sand.

The shovel pounds an area just to the left of my head.

"Why would you want to kill me anyway? I'm an idiot. I don't know anything."

"You know too much," Phone says.

"Seriously. What do I know?"

"Maybe we should find something else to do with him," Phone says.

"Like what?"

"Well, I mean part of the fun of this was that he would gain consciousness and find himself buried alive, thus dying in a suffocating way while he thinks about what he's done and why he's here. Now that he knows it's us doing the burying then he has some clue as to why he's being buried alive in the desert."

"Can I claw his face and rape him?"

"You bet. We'll give him a lot of Viagra so he doesn't have a choice."

"Sound good to you, Porky?"

It sounds terrible. I decide not to say anything except to ask, "What did I do?"

"Nothing," Phone says. "Nothing at all. Nothing ever."

I'm unburied, blindfolded, and thrown into the back of a truck.

Sometimes a Rape Shower Feels Like a Cliché

We get to the destination and they remove my blindfold, probably so I can be aware of the squalid nature of what's about to happen. They drag me inside. They're very rough. Unnecessarily so. Phone throws me down on the floor and shoves some kind of tube into my mouth. She shakes half a bottle of something into the tube and pours some water down it. I feel like throwing up but I'm afraid of what will happen if I do.

Estelle claws my face until it feels like bloody rags and then she rapes me while Phone menaces teenage Chloe with a knife. I liked it a lot better when I was mostly unconscious for this kind of thing. She rapes me for a really long time. Phone gets bored with the teenager and comes over to cheer on my orgasm but it's not working. Estelle gets tired and says she's afraid of breaking her hip again and Phone hops on. She only has to work for a few minutes before I come. Estelle disappears into a room of the trailer and I hear water running. She's probably taking a shower. I don't know how long it's been since I've taken a shower. It would probably feel really good but since I've just been raped it seems almost like a cliché.

Phone ties up my wrists and ankles and takes a seat in a recliner. She lights one of Estelle's long brown cigarettes and turns on the TV. The word SPACE flashes on the screen and Eldon Muntz is once again standing in front of the Grand Canyon. Buddy's rise to space is looped in the background, a comet of flame shooting upward. Maybe it's just a comet, a cheap science fiction effect.

"It is time for each of us to claim our home in space. The trash was just a metaphor for us—the poor, the disadvantaged. It is up to each of us to bypass the guards of the rich and fill the Grand Canyon with America's slave resources—ourselves. Join me. Join me."

Fill the Grand Canyon and Live Forever

I would think this sounds crazy except that I know exactly where he's coming from.

Estelle comes out of the shower wearing a bathrobe. She sits down on the worn couch next to Phone and lights a cigarette.

"We're going to have to get out of here," Phone says. She gestures at the TV which now just shows a flashing image of Muntz's face alternated with the phrase: WE ARE SPACE. "People are going to start throwing themselves into the Canyon. The military's not going to let that happen. We have liabilities." She gestures at me and Chloe with her cigarette.

"Back to Ohio?"

"No. That's too far."

"I'll make some calls."

Estelle goes into one of the back bedrooms to make some calls.

"Hey, Jackass," Phone says. I'm thinking she means me. "Don't freak out too much, okay? Whatever happens is going to happen. Nothing you can try to do will stop it. Got that? So just keep doing that fat lot of nothing you've been doing."

"I'm not talking to you anymore."

"Real mature."

"I can't believe you were in cahoots with Estelle."

"Girls have to stick together."

"What about her?" I nod toward Chloe.

"She'll come around. Once she realizes what's good for her."

"You people are sick."

"No. We're just better than you."

Estelle comes out of the bedroom. Now she's wearing the stripper clothes I'm more used to seeing her in. "Be here in a few."

"Awesome," Phone says.

Estelle goes into the kitchen, grabs a steak knife, crouches down next to me and starts carving. "You know," she says in a moment of contemplation. "I'm thinking we take him back and sacrifice him."

"It's up to you. I'm done with him."

She flips to a news station. The elevator factory is on the news. The tall part where they tested the elevators was smashed. A smoldering private jet lies off to the side. They show a picture of Mr. Elevator and say he was the alleged pilot. It doesn't make a whole lot of sense but neither does the dollar sign Estelle's carving into my forearm.

They're loading the devastated part of the building into a massive dump truck and I again think of all the trash filled vehicles continuing their pilgrimage to the Grand Canyon. I think about what

Phone said about the military stepping it up if people start throwing themselves in. Would soldiers shoot them just to keep them from fulfilling what might be a great sense of purpose? Will being shot make the jumpers feel more special? These thoughts, these questions. They don't have answers. At least, I don't think they do. I think I would rather jump to my death than be shot. Jumping is solitary, personal.

Phone drags me outside while Estelle douses the trailer in gasoline. A helicopter descends from the sky just as Estelle is setting the trailer ablaze.

"Isn't Chloe still in there?" I ask.

"Yeah, so? You wanna go in after her?"

I really don't but decide not to say anything so I don't seem so complicit.

The helicopter makes a rough landing. It has a vanity plate on the front that says: SLADE FTW.

We board the chopper. The pilot doesn't say anything. Ghastly, fleshy things line the windshield of the chopper.

Phone, noticing my gaze, says, "Throats," and I decide to leave it at that.

The helicopter lifts into the air and I'm almost sure, over the roar of the blades, I can hear Chloe screaming from the trailer.

The chopper pilot growls, "Someone should have ripped that bitch's throat out."

Sometimes a Place is Just a Place

I'm not sure how long the helicopter ride is. Estelle beats me mercilessly the entire time. The chopper pilot hoots and cheers her on. He gets especially excited when there's blood. Phone sleeps or maybe she's just sitting with her eyes closed and contemplating everything. Sometimes she's typing into an expensive smartphone I don't remember her having before. After what feels like days, the pilot shouts, "Get ready! Get ready!" and Estelle and Phone don parachutes. This doesn't bode very well for me. They each grab one of my arms and then dive out of the helicopter and we're plummeting through the air. When they pull their cords, I feel pretty sure I'm going to just keep plummeting but their grips must be pretty good and I don't. We land in a heap on the ground. Estelle pulls a large knife from her stripper boot and severs the cords. We're in the middle of a large field.

A black van hurtles toward us. I'm blindfolded again and shoved into the van when it pulls to a stop.

We rumble through the blackness. We could be anywhere. Still blindfolded, I'm led out of the van into a stifling blanket of moist heat. We then go up a number of stairs and stop. I think I hear a doorbell in the distance. We must be at somebody's house. Or apartment. Who has that many stairs leading to their front door? If it were an apartment, we would have probably gone inside before climbing the stairs. The door creaks open.

"Yes?" a very proper voice says.

"He should be expecting us."

I wait for some kind of questioning response. Instead, a voice booms from deeper in the house. "Ah, Estelle! Persephone! I've been waiting for you. Come in. Come in."

Fill the Grand Canyon and Live Forever

Even before we're over the threshold, I can feel the chill of the air conditioning wafting out. I'm expecting that gross burnt carpet smell like that time in Estelle's friend's apartment. Instead it smells like flowers, peonies or something, with the underlying scent of food. I'm so hungry I want to follow the food smell.

"We've brought you an offering," Phone says.

"Hmmm," the man says. "I usually like them younger and ... female ... and definitely thinner."

"This is a sacrificial offering. For dinner."

"Oh! Well, in that case, splendid!"

"Should we drug him," Estelle barks.

"No," Phone says. "We'll want him conscious for it. Do you have somewhere we can put him?"

"Right up the stairs there. First door on the right."

I'm led up the stairs, through a door, and onto a bed. I'm handcuffed to what I'm assuming is a bedpost and I hear the door click shut.

I'm asleep in a matter of seconds.

I Dream of Nothing

I wish I had some sort of dream that explained everything but my body and brain are so thirsty for sleep that I dream of nothing.

I have no idea how long it is before I'm awoken to raucous laughter and the removal of the blindfold.

The World is Mostly About Slavery and Death

I'm looking at a bald man wearing sunglasses, an earpiece, and an expensive black suit. All the laughter and commotion is coming from some place farther away. Downstairs maybe. Punctuating the laughter are screams and shouts of terror. The bald man makes a gesture for me to stand up. I do, but the handcuffs are keeping me close to the bed. The man karate chops the chain and snaps it.

"Follow me," he says.

I follow him out of the room and into a long hallway. My legs feel weak. I fight the urge to look around. It almost looks like I'm in a very expensive hotel. I'm led to the end of the hall. Past several doors. Perverse laughter, screaming, and whimpering are coming from behind nearly every door. I become even more suspicious of the doors that hold silence. At the end of the hall we turn to the right and go up another flight of stairs. At the top is something like a lobby complete with a receptionist's desk and everything. No one is behind the desk. There is only a set of double doors on this floor. I follow the man to the doors and he gives two quick knocks.

"Come in. Come in." Probably the owner of this mansion.

The man is seated behind a large desk. It's startling. The man is Mr. Elevator. I wouldn't have recognized his voice. Estelle and Phone are seated on the near side of the desk. They look cleaned up. Phone is still wearing a cheerleading outfit but it looks new and is mostly black with a few red accents. *She* looks clean, also. Estelle is wearing an elegant ball gown but she still looks old and vicious.

"Have a seat, Mr. Boring."

I take a seat, feeling especially filthy. Estelle and Phone even *smell* good.

"Mr. Elevator?" I say.

He laughs. "You must be thinking of my brother, Mr. Elevator East. He's dead. Perhaps you've seen the news although I imagine you've been quite busy. I'm Mr. Elevator West."

"I did see something about that."

"No matter. It's not like the world needs more elevators. The whole theory of ascension is a moot point now anyway. The future is all about leveling, cutting down. Right? Except for a few."

Behind Mr. Elevator West is a whole wall of monitors, all of them turned off.

"Sure, whatever," I say, now distracted by the monitors.

"I'm one of those few, Mr. Boring. See, my brother had it all wrong. You know he dreamed of building an elevator that went to space. He thought there would be money in that. Exploration." Mr. Elevator West laughs. He plucks up a small remote control that has been resting on the corner of his desk. "But who would be able to afford an elevator to space? Only the very rich, right?"

"Sure."

"But we're interested in other things. Not space. We know there's nothing there. Oh I'm sure there are some resources or what not, but leave that for the young and eager. We're interested in more earthly desires."

He presses a button on the remote control and all of the monitors come on at once. I'm amazed at the similarity of the images on the screens, even though they are all different. Fat white men looming over beds, sometimes two to a room. Most of the beds contain a very young girl or boy.

"I own everyone on those screens, Mr. Boring, both the young and the older. I could go into specifics but I'm assuming you don't really care and you look too poor and stupid to understand, anyway. What you're probably wondering is why you're here."

"Sure. I guess."

"You are here to make a choice. A survival choice. Are you ready for your options? It'll be fun!"

"Sure."

"One: You can stay here and work for me. I would let you live. You would occasionally get to indulge yourself." He motions to the monitors behind him but I'm finding the things displayed on them very tough to watch. And while there's a base part of me thinking it wouldn't be so bad to be one of them, to have innocent girls served up on a plate whenever I wanted them, there's another part of me that realizes this is just a base instinct and it's a sign of cooperation and civilization to deny a lot of those base instincts. And most of these base instincts bring dire consequences. In this case there was an obvious legality issue not to mention the prospect of somehow being indentured or owned by Mr. Elevator West. "Two: You can try to escape. I can't promise what will happen if you do this. You might find a gap. You might make it past the guests, and the armed guards and the dogs and the electric fence and the occasional landmine. You might not. If not, the end result will be horrendous and drawn out, I can assure you. But if you do make it out, you'll have complete freedom. I'll even deposit a healthy sum of cash into your bank account every month. You probably won't ever have to work again. But, in short, you have to play the game and you have to win. Or third: You can serve as Estelle and Persephone originally intended, i.e. a human sacrifice. The end result is obvious—death. But you won't have the possible guilt and subservience associated with option one and you won't have the inevitable pain and torture possible with option number two. If it were up to me, the choice is obvious. I'll give you a couple of minutes to decide."

He swivels around in his chair to watch the monitors.

I look at Estelle and she's smirking at me. I look at Phone but her gaze is also on the monitors, something like glazed longing or possibly even fear in her eyes. Neither one of them are going to be any help.

Life is Some Kind of Joke

Option one is not an option. I've done some pretty despicable things in my life, many of them undoubtedly consumed by the black holes in my brain, but I can't do what Mr. Elevator West suggests. Option three seems a lot like suicide, which goes against my life philosophy. It's at this point I even realize I have a life philosophy. Life is some kind of joke. Possibly a cruel one. But you have to stick around for the punch line. That left option two. I'm about ready to tell him that's the one I'll go with when Phone surreptitiously moves a hand over to my knee and gives it a squeeze. She squeezes my leg two more times. Three. Option three. Sacrifice. Phone. Really? How can I trust Phone? Of course, if I do trust Phone and say option three then it's not really suicide because I wouldn't see death as an outcome. I would see something else. Something unknown. I try to make eye contact with her, try to get some kind of reassurance from her, but she's still staring at the atrocities happening on the screens.

I clear my throat and give Mr. Elevator West my answer.

It Might End Like This

I'm given a lavish bath by a number of servants. Once finished, I'm amazingly hairless. Since I've volunteered to be their sacrifice for the evening, I feel entitled to at least one favor.

I wander around until I find one of the servants.

He punches me in the stomach, hard, and I collapse to the ground.

"I'd like to ask a favor."

He grunts.

"I need to get online and say bye to a few people and then jerk off to porn one last time. If you can't allow me this, I'm afraid I'm going to have to alter my choice."

He walks off.

I walk back to the bedroom I came from and sprawl on the bed. I'm still naked but I don't really care. It seems like a petty thing to be worried about at this time.

Eventually someone comes into the room with a laptop. I open it up and check my sales figures. Strangely, *Dick Swap* has sold -1. I don't see how this is possible and I'm momentarily furious. I go to my MyFace page. I wonder what Chuck is up to. His friend count is really high. Eighty million. I find a video of the Grand Canyon commercial with Muntz. There are several of them and I watch them a couple of times each. They don't really make a lot of sense. I watch a couple of the MeTube videos and remember the sense of purpose I had when first watching them. I'm not even sure why it would matter if the Grand Canyon was filled. Buddy was already tossed in the Canyon and maybe rejuvenated before returning to space. Maybe not. Am I hoping to be thrown in the Grand Canyon? It sounds like I'll be eaten so there won't be any flesh on my bones. I can't really find any in depth information on dying, being thrown into the Grand

Canyon, and being brought back to life. I copy the video and paste it onto Chuck's page. I start browsing for porn and within a few seconds Chuck sends me a message that says: "Do it."

I'm not really sure what this means.

I think about it while I continue to browse for pornography.

Four servants wearing expensive suits enter the room. They're also bald, wearing sunglasses and earpieces.

"I haven't even found a video good enough to jerk off to yet."

One of the servants throws the laptop into the corner of the room. It doesn't break or anything. Just lands there.

They pick me up and carry me through a series of rooms and corridors. They're big guys and I wonder if it really takes four of them to carry me or if they're just being insulting.

I'm strapped to some kind of slab covered in a black velvety cloth. They lift up the slab or maybe it's a sacrificial altar and begin walking me through the house. It seems only fitting that I'm heading for a possible death since I've been treated better in the last hour or so than I have been in a very long time.

They take me toward the back of the house and through elaborate double doors held open by two more servants and then we are outside and it's dark and hot and humid. If I lift my head I can see all the guests, dressed in expensive suits and gowns, shimmering everywhere. Their skin seems to shimmer as much as the watches and jewelry hanging from their wrists and necks and fingers. Mr. Elevator West waits in the center, beaming and holding a long curved knife. I'm placed on a marble slab and I think *this* is probably the sacrificial altar. I try to scan the grinning faces for Phone. I see Estelle standing close to Mr. Elevator West. She looks like a ravenous jackal. Maybe she's filed her dentures down to points. No Phone anywhere. My blood is pounding in my ears.

"I know you are all hungry," Mr. Elevator West says. "And I apologize for making you wait this long but didn't I tell you it would be worth it!" It's like he's talking to employees at a company picnic or something. They all laugh and applaud politely. A few guests, probably the drunkest ones, whistle.

The appreciation dies down and Mr. Elevator says, "I don't see any reason to delay this any longer."

He raises the sacrificial knife and moves closer to me. I try to say something but my mouth doesn't want to work. I think about closing my eyes but that feels weak. I place my head back on the altar and stare up at the night sky. It's humid and hazy so I can only see one star. Maybe the North Star? Isn't that supposed to be Venus or something? It looks like the star's getting bigger but I just attribute that to the same whatever that's keeping my mouth from working. Nerves or expensive drugs or something. But no, it's definitely getting bigger, and possibly even descending at an alarmingly quick rate. There's a ripple of noise running through the guests and when I look away from whatever is in the sky I see that many of them are looking up. Once the others realize something is going on, they turn their heads up too. Eventually even Mr. Elevator West lowers the sacrificial knife and joins them.

The ball gets bigger and bigger and now I can hear it too.

Buddy? I think.

The guests are all transfixed and I try to get up from the altar, thinking maybe this is what Phone wanted. Maybe this was my chance to escape, but I can't move. I feel locked into place.

The guests' wide-eyed awe quickly turns to screams of terror as they realize the ball of light is not going to stop and isn't as far away as they thought it was.

It's amazingly bright, so bright I can't keep looking at it, and then I'm closing my eyes and I'm hearing screams everywhere and I feel it slam into me, driving spikes of heat into every pore of my body.

I'm floating up above it all. When I look down I see the mansion burning and guests running around, on fire and screaming. Off in the distance, near the woods, I see a line of children led by Phone, heading into the woods.

I'm not sure where I'm going, if I'm dead or not. I feel pretty good about things. I tell myself this. I'm not sure if it's true.

The sun is just starting to come up and from this altitude it looks amazing. I run my hands over my body just to make sure I still have one. It feels like I do and it feels pretty much the same, still completely hairless. Kind of fat. Penis, small. I don't mind where I am right now and I don't know how long it lasts.

I look down. Roads and highways crisscross the United States. For as far as I can see, those roads and highways are clogged with trucks and cars – big and small – all laden with trash.

I realize I'm flying but I have no control over my direction. It's obvious where I'm going. Ground Zero. Back to the Grand Canyon. I see it below me and I'm slowly coming down in the blue dawn. Trucks line the various rims of the Canyon, dumping trash. Some of it is really questionable. One guy has a truck full of various skulls. Another truck might contain dead babies. I try to convince myself they're dolls. Phone is running around. She looks happier. She's cheering on the people in their trash dumping endeavors. Agatha is there. She's wearing like a billion coats, taking them off and throwing them in one by one. I think about how we drifted apart. Everyone drifts apart. And then, sometimes, they come together again but they're never the same. Sometimes they're better. Sometimes they're not.

I scan the blue sky and think of Buddy. Maybe he made this possible.

Fill the Grand Canyon and Live Forever

I'm still trying to figure out what "this" is. It seems like a good thing. A bunch of people getting together and getting rid of everything. Becoming savage. Maybe once the Canyon is full, we'll roam into the hillsides and gather in packs and storm the homes and the gated communities and yachts of the rich.

Part of me thinks that sounds beautiful and part of me thinks it sounds like the apocalypse.

Maybe it could be both and that might not be a bad thing.

I'm standing at the rim of the Canyon. I wonder if anyone else has thrown themselves in yet. I wonder what will happen. I look down and I feel my brain become nothing, dissolving, consumed by the cracks and holes. Doctor Blast stands to my right. I remember him saying he once encouraged a man to jump through a window and it took him years before he hit the ground. Jumping is action. Jumping is something. A few years might be all I have. But hitting the ground is inevitable. Everyone has to hit the bottom at some point.

Dan Banal Goes to the Grand Canyon

Dan Banal, in weekend gear, stands next to his wife. Both of them stare out at the Grand Canyon. No one else is around. It seems exceptionally empty. Everything seems exceptionally empty.

"Sure is big," Dan says.

"It sure is," his wife says.

"Goes down far."

"Really far."

"Beautiful."

"Majestic."

"Thrilling."

Dan reaches into his pocket and pulls out a nondescript piece of trash. He holds it out and turns his hand over so it flutters down into the Canyon.

"Well, what now?" he says.

"We could go on one of those donkey rides."

"I'd rather not."

"We could go back home."

"Yeah. Let's do that. This was a good trip."

"It was great."

"The best."